Contents

*Dedicated to the belief that we can
all do better, be better, live better.
We owe our best to each
and every child.*

GHOSt BOYs

Jewell Parker Rhodes

OXFORD
UNIVERSITY PRESS

Great Clarendon Street, Oxford, OX2 6DP, United Kingdom

Oxford University Press is a department of the University of Oxford. It furthers the University's objective of excellence in research, scholarship, and education by publishing worldwide. Oxford is a registered trade mark of Oxford University Press in the UK and in certain other countries.

Text © Jewell Parker Rhodes, 2018

Additional resources © Oxford University Press 2022

The moral rights of the author have been asserted.

First published in Great Britain in 2018 by Hodder and Stoughton.

This educational edition published in 2022.

British Library Cataloguing in Publication Data

Data available

ISBN 978-1-38-2036399

1 3 5 7 9 10 8 6 4 2

Paper used in the production of this book is a natural, recyclable product made from wood grown in sustainable forests.

The manufacturing process conforms to the environmental regulations of the country of origin.

Printed in Great Britain by CPI Group (UK) Ltd., Croydon CR0 4YY

Acknowledgements

The publisher and author would like to thank the following for permission to use photographs and other copyright material:

Cover: Shadra Strickland

Photos: p195; JUSTIN TALLIS/AFP via Getty Images

Artwork: Shadra Strickland and Oxford University Press

The author and publisher would like to thank Julie Moxton for writing the additional resources.

The resources on pages 196-200 have been developed using insight from the Oxford Children's Corpus and Oxford Children's Dictionaries Team.

DEAD

How small I look. Laid out flat, my stomach touching ground. My right knee bent and my brand-new Nikes stained with blood.

I stoop and stare at my face, my right cheek flattened on concrete. My eyes are wide open. My mouth, too.

I'm dead.

I thought I was bigger. Tough. But I'm just a bit of nothing.

My arms are outstretched like I was trying to fly like Superman.

I'd barely turned, sprinting. *Pow, pow.* Two bullets. Legs gave way. I fell flat. Hard.

I hit snowy ground.

Ma's running. She's wailing, 'My boy. My boy.' A policeman holds her back. Another policeman is standing over me, murmuring, 'It's a kid. It's a kid.' Ma's struggling. She gasps like she can't breathe; she falls to her knees and screams.

I can't bear the sound.

Sirens wail. Other cops are coming. Did someone call an ambulance?

I'm still dead. Alone on the field. The policeman closest to me is rubbing his head. In his hand, his gun dangles.

The other policeman is watching Ma like she's going to hurt someone. Then, he shouts, 'Stay back!'

People are edging closer, snapping pictures, taking video with their phones. 'Stay back!' The policeman's hand covers his holster.

More people come. Some shout. I hear my name. 'Jerome. It's Jerome.' Still, everyone stays back. Some curse; some cry.

Doesn't seem fair. Nobody ever paid me any attention. I skated by. Kept my head low.

Now I'm famous.

Chicago Tribune
OFFICER: 'I HAD NO CHOICE!'

Jerome Rogers, 12, shot at abandoned Green Street lot. Officer says, 'He had a gun.'

ALIVE

December 8
Morning

'Come straight home. You hear me, Jerome? Come straight home.'

'I will.' I always do.

Ma leans down, hugs me. Grandma slides another stack of pancakes on my plate. 'Promise?'

'Promise.' Same ritual every day.

I stuff a pancake into my mouth. Kim sticks out her tongue.

I'm the good kid. Wish I wasn't. I've got troubles but I don't get *in* trouble. Big difference.

I'm pudgy, easily teased. But when I'm a grown-up, everybody's going to be my friend. I might even be president. Like Obama.

Kim says she believes me. That's why I put up with her.

She can be annoying. Asking too many questions. Like: 'What makes a cloud?' 'Why're their shapes different?' Telling me: '*Minecraft* is stupid.' Begging me to help pick out a library book.

'Hurry up. Else you'll be late,' says Grandma. She hands Ma a lunch sack. At school, me and Kim get free lunch.

Everybody works in our house. Ma is a receptionist at Holiday Inn. Her shift starts at eight a.m.

Me and Kim's job, says Ma, is going to school.

Pop leaves the house at four a.m. He's a sanitation officer. He drives a truck. In the old days, there was a driver and two men hanging off the truck's sides, leaping down to lift and dump smelly trash cans. Now steel arms pick up bins. Pop does the whole route by himself. He stays in the air-conditioned cabin, steering, pressing the button for the mechanical arm, and listening to Motown. The Temptations. Smokey Robinson. The Supremes. Sixties pop music. Lame. Hip-hop is better.

Grandma keeps house. She cooks, cleans. Makes it so me and Kim aren't home alone. Have snacks. Homework help (though I prefer playing video games).

'After school is troublesome,' says Ma.

Pushing back my chair, I kiss her.

'Come straight home,' Ma repeats, tucking in her white uniform shirt.

Grandma hugs, squeezes me like I'm a balloon. She pecks my cheek. 'I'm worried about you. Been having bad dreams.'

'Don't worry.' That's my other job – comforting Ma and Grandma. Grandma worries the most. She has dreams. 'Premonitions,' she calls them. Worries about bad things happening. But I don't know what, where, when, or why.

'Sometimes I dream lightning strikes. Or earthquakes. Sometimes it's dark clouds mushrooming in the sky. I wake troubled.'

Remembering her words, I worry. I know Ma will remind her to take her blood pressure pill.

Pop worries, too, but he usually doesn't say so. Early morning, before he leaves for work, he always stops by my room. (Kim's, too.)

He opens the door; there's a shaft of hallway light. I've gotten used to it. Eyes closed, I pretend to be asleep. Pop looks and looks, then softly closes the door and goes to work.

'Jerome?' Grandma clasps my shoulder. 'Tell me three good things.'

I pause. Grandma is truly upset. Half-moon shadows rim her eyes.

'Three, Jerome. Please.'

Three. Grandma's special number. 'Three means "All". Optimism. Joy,' Grandma says every day. 'Heaven, Earth, Water. Three means you're close to the angels.'

I lick my lip. 'One, school is fun.' Hold up two fingers. 'I like it when it snows.' Then, 'Three, when I'm grown, I'm going to have a cat.' (A dog, too. But I don't say that. A dog would be *four* good things. Can't ruin the magical three.)

Grandma exhales. I've said exactly what she needed to hear. *Fine*, I've told her. *I'm fine.*

I stuff my books into my bag. I wink, wave bye to Ma.

'Study hard,' she says, both smiling and frowning. She's happy I comforted Grandma, but unhappy with Grandma's Southern ways.

Ma wants me and Kim to be 'ED – YOU – CATED.' She pokes her finger at us when she says 'YOU'.

'ED – YOU' – *poke* – 'CATED, Jerome.' Sometimes the poke hurts a bit. But I get it.

Grandma dropped out of elementary school to care for her younger sisters. Ma and Pop finished high school. Me and Kim are supposed to go to college.

Kim is by the front door, backpack slung over her shoulder. Kim's nice. But I don't tell her that. She's bony, all elbows and knees. When she's a teenager, I'll be grown. Everybody will worry more about her than me.

Ma always says, 'In this neighbourhood, getting a child to adulthood is perilous.'

I looked up the word. *Perilous.* 'Risky, dangerous.'

I pull Kim's braid. Frowning, she swats my hand.

Can't be good all the time.

Later, I'll take my allowance and buy Kim a book. Something scary, fun.

*   *   *

We walk to school. Not too fast like we're running; not too slow like we're daring someone to stop us. Our walk has got to be just right.

Green Street isn't peaceful; it isn't green either. Just brick houses, some lived in, some abandoned. Out-of-work men play cards on the street, drinking beer from cans tucked in paper bags.

Eight blocks to travel between home and school.

On the fifth block from our house is Green Acres. A meth lab exploded there and two houses burnt. Neighbours tried to clear the debris, make a basketball court. It's pathetic. A hoop without a net. Spray-painted lines. Planks of wood hammered into sad bleachers. At least somebody tried.

Two blocks from school, drug dealers slip powder or pill packets to customers, stuffing cash into their pockets. Pop says, 'Not enough jobs, but still, it's wrong. Drugs kill.' Me and Kim cross the street, away from the dealers. They're not the worst, though. School bullies are the worst. Bullies never leave you alone. Most days I try to stay near adults. Lunchtime I hide in the locker room, the supply closet, or the bathroom.

Kim slips her hand in mine. She knows.

'I'll meet you after school,' I say.

'You always do.' She squeezes my palm. 'You going to have a good day?'

'Yeah,' I say, trying to smile, searching the sidewalks for Eddie, Snap, and Mike. They like to dump my backpack. Push me, pull my pants down. Hit me upside the head.

Kim clenches her hand, purses her lips. She's smart for a third grader. She knows surviving the school day isn't easy for me.

She never tells.

Ma, Pop, and Grandma have enough to worry about. They know Kim's popular and I'm not. But they don't need to know I'm being bullied.

'Kimmeee!' a girl shouts.

Kim flashes me a grin. I nod. Then she skips up the school steps, her braids bouncing as she and Keisha chatter-giggle, crossing left into the elementary school. Middle school is to the right.

'Yo, Jerome.'

I look over my shoulder, hugging my backpack closer. Mike's grinning. Eddie and Snap, fists clenched, thug-posing, stand by his side. Damn. Have to be super careful.

During lunch, I'll hide in the bathroom. Maybe they'll forget about me? Find another target?

I can hope.

Just like I hope I'll win the lottery. A million dollars.

DEAD

GHOST

The apartment is packed. Ma's sisters, Uncle Manny, my cousins. Reverend Thornton. The kitchen table is covered with food – my favourites, potato salad, lemon meringue pie, pork chops. If everyone wasn't so sad-faced, I'd swear it was a party.

I reach for a cornbread square and my hand passes through it. Weird, but it's okay. I'm not hungry. I guess I'll never be hungry again.

I move, circling the living room.

People don't pass through me. It's like they sense I'm taking up space. Even though they can't see me, they shift, lean away. I'm glad about that. It's enough being dead without folks entering and leaving me like in *Ghostbusters*.

Ma is in my bedroom, lying on my bed with orange basketball sheets. A poster of Stephen Curry shooting a ball is taped on the wall.

Ma's eyes are swollen. Grandma holds her hand like she's a little girl.

I don't feel much – like I'm air touching the furniture or Ma's hand. Maybe that's what happens

19

when you're dead? But seeing Ma crying makes me want to crush, slam something into the ground. *Inside me* hurts; *outside me* feels nothing. I try to touch her – *nothing* – just like the cornbread. Ma shivers and it makes me sad that I can't comfort her.

I turn towards the doorway. Kim is reading a book. She does that when gunshots are fired outside, when our upstairs neighbours, Mr and Mrs Lyon, are fighting, yelling. For now, I know she's okay. Reading makes her feel better.

I stand in the doorway, shocked how my room is filled with family, how it isn't my room any more. Isn't my place where I imagine, dream I'm playing college ball. Or in the army, diving out of aeroplanes. Or rapping on the radio. Or being president.

To my right, Pop leans into the corner. Like he wants to collapse into the space and disappear. His eyes are closed and his arms are folded across his chest. Who will he shoot hoops with? Or eat hot dogs with while cheering the Chicago Bears?

'I'm here. I'm still here,' I rasp.

Ma, on my bed, curls on her side; Pop's lips tighten. Grandma looks up, searching.

'I'm still here, Grandma.'

Her face is a wrinkled mess. I didn't realise it before, but Grandma is really old. She looks up and through me. Her eyes glimmer; she nods. *Does she see? Does she see me?*

Reverend Thornton moves past me. He doesn't realise he's tucking his stomach in and entering the room sideways. Grandma notices. Nobody else thinks it's strange.

'We should pray,' he says.

'What for?' asks Pop. 'Jerome's not coming back.'

Ma gasps, sits up. 'James. We don't know God's will.'

'It's man's will – it's a policeman acting a fool. Murdering my boy.' Pop's fist slams the wall. The drywall cracks. I've never seen Pop violent.

'He's in a better place,' says Reverend. 'Jerome's in a better place.'

Am I?

Ma rocks, her arms crossed over her stomach.

'Every goodbye ain't gone,' says Grandma.

'Mom, hush with that nonsense,' complains Ma.

'Every black person in the South knows it's true. Dead, living, no matter. Both worlds are close. Spirits aren't gone.'

'Superstition,' scoffs Reverend. 'This is Chicago. Jerome's soul is already gone.'

I kneel. 'I'm still here, Ma. I'm still here.'

'We'll bury him tomorrow,' cries Ma, and I want to cry, too, though my eyes don't make tears any more.

'Sue, I'm going to sue,' says Pop. 'No sense why my boy's dead and those white men are walking around alive. Free.'

'Emmett. Just like Emmett Till,' says Grandma. 'He was a Chicago boy, too.'

'This isn't 1955,' says Reverend, calming.

'Tamir Rice, then,' shouts Pop. '2014. He died in Cleveland. Another boy shot just because he's black.'

Grandma looks at the space where I'm standing. Her head is cocked sideways; she's breathing soft.

'No justice. No peace,' says Pop. 'Since slavery, white men been killing blacks.' Then, he starts to cry. Ma hugs him and they hold tight to each other like they're both going to drown.

My heart shatters. Nothing hurt this much, not even the bullets searing my back.

My alarm clock clicks: twelve a.m. Nine hours ago I was playing in Green Acres.

Now it's a new day. I'm here but not here.

Where's my body? Where do they keep it until it's laid in the ground?

'Time to wake up.'

I spin around. Who said that?

I leave the bedroom, wandering through the apartment, past eating, crying, praying people, searching for who spoke to me.

In the kitchen, by the window, I see a brown boy like me. His eyes are black velvet. He's tall as me; his hair, short like mine. He stares and stares as if the world has made him so sorry, so sad.

Scared, I step backwards. He nods, like he expected it; then, disappears.

He's not in the kitchen. My hands pass through the glass pane. I see the starry night sky, the darkened road, street lamps attracting bugs.

Across the street, I see him. Wispy like soft rain. *A ghost?*

Like me?

CHURCH

It's awful spending days in the apartment, everybody angry and mourning. Awful not being able to lie on my bed. Or eat. Or speak.

I can't sleep. No rest for the dead.

I watch my family crying, talking in whispers. Ma seems like she's sleepwalking – shuffling about the apartment like she's still looking for me. Pop is always shouting into the phone. Talking to lawyers, newspaper folks. I can't think of anything worse than watching my family hurt.

At night, the living room fills with shadows. Misshapen, ugly things. I don't go into my bedroom. Too sad. Ma sleeps there now. Kim, whose bed is the couch, whimpers while she dreams. Afraid to sleep, Grandma stares at the ceiling. Pop, tangled in sheets, sleeps on his back, both arms crossed over his eyes.

No one rests well.

Is there some place I'm supposed to go? I hope it's heaven. A good place. But I'm still here – which is nowhere, not able to help anybody.

Grandma hums gospel and wherever I move, she seems to know. She looks at me standing near the television. She turns when I follow Ma into the kitchen. She leans forward, humming louder when I sit on the chair beside Pop.

If she could *really* see me, I'd be alive and she'd be telling me to 'clean my room', 'take out the trash', 'wash my hands'. I miss her ordering me to do chores. Or saying, 'Homework. No TV.'

Today, Ma, Pop, Kim, and Grandma dress for church. It's my funeral. I sit with them in a black Cadillac – it's the nicest car I've ever been in.

'An open casket,' murmurs Ma. '"I want the whole world to see what they did to my boy." Isn't that what Mrs Till said? Isn't it?'

Grandma gets out of the car first, then Kim, Ma, Pop. Then me. Grandma whispers at the air, 'Time to get going, boy. Time to move on.'

I'm stunned hearing Grandma speak to me. But I can't move on. I don't know how. Or where to move on to. How am I supposed to know how to be dead?

I follow them up the steps. Kim reaches for Pop to pick her up. He does and she buries her face in his neck.

'Señor Rogers. Sir, sir.' It's Carlos. My new friend. (Old friend now.)

Pop doesn't hear him – he's busy comforting Kim – but Grandma does. She waves Carlos to her. Wiping tears, he hands her a piece of paper. Grandma looks at it. She presses the paper to her heart, then hugs Carlos – a big stomach-crushing hug, the kind she used to give me when she was happiest.

The thick church doors open.

Organ music swells. 'Amazing Grace', Grandma's favourite.

Carlos runs down the steps. He's still wearing a hoodie. Never mind the cold and snow.

Deacons and church ladies in white dresses swarm about my family, fanning them, guiding them from the vestibule into the church.

I start to follow. Suddenly, my ghost friend is beside me.

'Don't go in there. You don't want to see.'

'Who're you?'

'Someone I wish you didn't know.'

I stare. His skin is paper-thin, dull. His shoulders are broad; his cheekbones, high. His clothes are funny. Old-timey. He's wearing a white shirt with a tie. He holds a rimmed hat.

'I'm you.'

Nothing makes sense. I reach out to touch him. *Maybe ghosts can touch ghosts?*

He disappears.

I sit on the church steps. Stay outside.

Maybe it's better this way? Not seeing myself in a casket. I try to imagine what Carlos wanted to give Pop. What Grandma saw.

What would, just for a second, make Grandma happy at my funeral?

ALIVE

December 8
School

Mr Myers is one of only two men who teach in the whole middle school. I know he wasn't a cool kid. He keeps making it hard for us uncool kids. It's like he didn't learn anything growing up.

Right now, he's introducing a new student. Seriously. Like standing in front of the class is going to make you feel welcome. It's like giving a kid a sign saying KICK ME. The new kid knows. He looks grim. He wears baggy jeans and a hoodie. His hood's up. Mr Myers pulls it down and you can see curly black, shoulder-length hair, almost like a girl's. I groan.

'Carlos is from San Antonio, Texas,' chimes Mr Myers. 'He's lucky. He had classes in Spanish and English.

'Eddie, you speak Spanish, don't you?'

'I speak Dominican. Don't know Texas Spanish.'

Everyone in the class snickers. Carlos's face reddens.

Mr Myers blinks. 'It'd be nice if everyone helped Carlos feel welcome here in Chicago.'

Everyone groans. Mr Myers is making everything worse – making him stand out, be needy, expecting us kids to help when all we want to do is survive.

Hopeful, Mr Myers scans the room.

Carlos looks like he's going to cry. He's not tough enough for this school. I feel sorry for him.

'Hola,' I say, then wince. *What's the matter with me?*

Carlos smiles. Mr Myers acts like he wants to shake my hand. He points for Carlos to sit in a chair next to me.

There's always empty chairs near me.

I glance back at Eddie. He makes a fist, twisting it in his palm. He's going to kill me. It won't be as bad as Carlos's beating. New students are beat-down magnets.

In Chicago, some kids speak Spanish at home, never at school. On Parent Night, if Eddie has to speak Spanish to his mom, he covers his mouth and whispers. He thinks speaking Spanish in school isn't cool. He makes faces when his mom tries to talk with his teachers.

I wish I could speak another language. 'Hola' is all I know.

Truth is, I have enough trouble speaking the right words in English and not having crews like Eddie, Snap, and Mike picking on me, saying, 'Stuck-up.' 'Teacher's pet.' All because I don't act bored, disrespectful in class, or pushy, loud at break.

I wish I were done with middle school. I get tired of dreaming about how life's going to be different when I grow up. Right now, it's *stupid, stupid, stupid.*

'Hey. Hey!'

I walk faster, trying to escape Carlos.

'Lunch?'

Carlos tugs my arm. Dead winter, his hoodie isn't going to protect against the cold. I take pity on him. It's not his fault his family moved to Chicago.

'This is how you do it,' I say. 'Follow me.' I walk quick and Carlos follows me into the cafeteria. 'No mushy food. No plates.'

Carlos nods. Then, wary, he looks around for Eddie. I don't tell him Mike punches the hardest. Snap likes to bite.

'Don't slow me down,' I warn.

I cut the line; some kids howl; I don't care. Being patient during lunchtime can get me whipped. I grab a sandwich, apple, and carton of milk. Carlos does the same.

There's stitching on his T-shirt.

Our school gets all kinds of poor. There's a little bit poor, more poor, then poorer than poor.

My family's a little bit poor as long as both my parents work. Carlos's family might be worse.

I think: today is a red-hot EMERGENCY. Without Carlos, it'd just be yellow.

'Come on.' I run; Carlos follows, tripping up flights of stairs.

'Here.' The bathroom on the highest floor is nearly always empty. Kids like to walk down, not up.

Usually I take the stall furthest away, next to the window, but I let Carlos have it. 'Plant your feet on the seat. No one can see your shoes. Eat.'

Carlos stares at me like I'm crazy.

'It works.'

I go into the next stall, lock the door, and unwrap my sandwich. I listen close. After a minute, I hear Carlos unwrap his sandwich. I wonder if he got tuna fish?

'Thanks.'

'No problem.'

School toilets don't have covers. We both squat over toilet water eating sandwiches. My apple is in my pocket. Milk balances on the toilet paper roll. Funny, it feels better not doing this by myself. Less lonely.

'Bearden isn't a bad school,' I say, trying to be helpful.

'In San Antonio, school's always trouble. Everyone fights. Everyone's afraid. I hope it's better here.'

The tuna's dirt dry. I almost choke. 'We fight here, too,' I say, honest. 'That's why we have security guards. Metal detectors.'

I hear Carlos breathing. He knows what I'm saying.

Chicago is probably worse than San Antonio.

'I wasn't trying to lie, Carlos. Not really. I didn't want you to feel bad.'

Carlos laughs. 'It's okay. Maybe every school is bad? But, here? Lunch over a toilet? That's a new one.'

I laugh. What can I say? The bathroom is my favourite hiding place. No one looks for me here. Even if a kid comes in, they don't bother with the end stalls. I stay quiet until I hear a flush, hand washing, and the door swinging open and shut.

I smack the green stall. Carlos smacks back. *Smack… smack.* I add syncopated slaps. He does, too. *Slap-a-slap-slap.* I slap. He slaps. *Slap-slap-slap. Smack,* goes Carlos. *Smack. Smack. Slap.* Carlos hums, whistles.

Soon, we're playing a rhythm on the graffiti-covered stalls like we're playing bongos. I decide Carlos is cool. He's smart enough to latch on to me. If I was new, I'd latch on to someone, too.

'Amigo?' he asks, tentatively.

Friend? I'm not sure how to answer.

Middle school is like a country. Alliances are hard, dangerous. Other kids' fights become your fights. You have to worry about your friends' friends, their gangs on the streets and in school. Everyone's in a crew. Except me.

Sure, I get picked on – mostly when Mike, Eddie, and Snap are bored. I'm an easy target. They can bully me but not have to war with any friends. The only advantage of being lonely is not worrying about being anyone else's backup.

'Friend?' Carlos asks again. 'If this were San Antonio, I would've said hi to you.' He pauses. 'We can look out for each other.'

I shudder. I can't see his face. But I hear the hope. By fifth grade, I gave up on friends. It's pathetic. Seventh grade, Carlos is still hoping to be cool. To have a friend.

'I didn't want to move, but my dad's a foreman now. For River North Construction. It's a big deal. Good for my family. More money. My mom's having a baby.' Carlos quiets.

I can tell he's a worrier. His voice strains like mine. He probably tries to be good all the time, too.

Carlos blurts, 'I didn't have friends in San Antonio. It isn't fair to live in two different cities and not have any friends.'

'Yes,' I say, not believing myself. Not believing I'd risk it. 'Friends.'

We can't see each other's faces, but I know we're both smiling.

I think Mr Myers would be proud of me. Grandma, too.

'Sssh.' The bathroom door squeaks, then slams. *Whack.* Even though I can't see him, I sense, like me, Carlos freezes.

Rubber soles squeak, boots stomp (Mike!), and then *bam*, they hit a bathroom stall door. 'Empty,' hollers Snap.

Bam. Bam. Bam, bam.

Bam. They hit my stall door. It's locked. I see Snap's Air Jordans, Mike's boots. Eddie bends, trying to see in. I keep still. He can't see above the toilet's base.

Bam. The last door flies open. *No-no-noooooo.* Carlos didn't lock the stall door.

'Got you,' Eddie crows.

'Stop, stop.' Mike is dragging Carlos. I can see his legs kicking, hear him gripping, grasping, trying to cling on, stay in the stall. 'Leave me alone.'

I slide the lock. 'Leave him alone!' I holler.

Eddie pushes me and I fall on to the toilet, scrambling to stay dry.

Carlos is crying. I rush out, pulling Mike off him. Mike punches me. Eddie grabs my collar.

'Stop, leave him alone.'

'You're nothing in Chicago. Say it.' Snap twists Carlos's arm. 'Say it, "I'm nothing."'

Carlos glares.

'You're a jerk.' Snap twists harder. 'A pimple like Jerome.' Mike and Eddie laugh.

Angry, Carlos jerks free. His leg swings back. 'Don't,' I warn. Carlos kicks. Snap howls, grabs his knee. Carlos punches, but his fist barely hits Snap's shoulder.

Mike punches Carlos. He falls backwards. Then, Mike and Snap are both kicking Carlos. In the stomach. The head.

Carlos is twisting, his arms flailing. Eddie holds me back. I tug hard. 'I'm telling,' I scream. I don't care if I'm a snitch. 'I'm going to tell.'

Eddie slams me against the wall.

All three look at me, faces snarled. They're furious. They didn't expect me to stand up to them.

I'm shaking. At least Carlos isn't getting kicked. But they're going to hurt me. Really hurt me. Scared, I brace myself.

I'm not going to beg.

Eddie laughs. His goofy, creepy laugh. Mike shoves my shoulder. 'Don't tell anybody,' he threatens.

'Yeah,' adds Snap. 'You won't be telling anybody anything.'

'Muerto.'

We all turn. Carlos has a gun.

DEAD

Preliminary Hearing
Chicago Courthouse

April 18

It's April. I'm four months dead.

In the courthouse, I feel clammy and cold. Not weather cold, just empty cold. I'm stuck. Stuck in time. Stuck being dead.

Ma, Grandma, and Pop are in the courtroom's front row behind the prosecutor. Reporters, sketch artists, Reverend Thornton, officers, and community folks fill the rest of the seats. Right behind the lawyer's desk are a white woman and a girl, her daughter, maybe. Both have sandy-brown hair. Both look sad.

There's no jury – just empty seats.

The judge isn't tall, about the same height as my ma. She wears black shoes. Her nails are painted pink.

'Preliminary hearings,' she says, 'don't determine innocence or guilt. They determine whether there is enough evidence for a trial. Whether Officer Moore should be charged with murder.'

Seems lame to me. I'm dead, aren't I?

A policeman is sitting in the dock, below the judge's chair. He has sandy-brown hair, too. Glazed, blue eyes. A lawyer is saying something to him but he's not listening, just looking at the woman and girl. His family, I think.

'Officer Moore, can you answer the question?'

'Sir?' The officer looks at the slim man.

'Were you in fear for your life?'

'Yes, yes. He had a gun.'

'Were you surprised later when the gun turned out to be a toy?'

'Yes. It looked real. He was threatening me.'

I shake my head. I never pointed a gun at the policeman. I walk closer to the officer. *Why's he telling lies?*

The girl in the front row points at me, whispers to her mother. I look at the girl, her eyes wide with fear. Like her dad was scared of me?

Her mother shushes her. Shoves her hand down.

The prosecutor continues, 'How old was the assailant?'

'I thought at least twenty-five. He was a man. A dangerous man.'

'So you were doing your job as trained?'

'Yes.'

'Were you upset to discover the man was a boy? A twelve-year-old boy?'

Ma starts moaning, crying, soft yet sharp.

'I was surprised. He was big, hulking. Scary.'

'You felt threatened?'

The officer pauses. I'm staring right into his eyes. He looks through me. He's studying his wife and daughter. His daughter is studying me. I don't know why or how she sees me.

He swallows, his tongue licking his bottom lip. 'I...felt...threatened.'

Pop stands, shouting, 'A grown man. Two grown men. You. Your partner, Officer Whitter. Armed. Threatened by a boy?'

Ma wails.

The woman judge pounds her gavel. 'Quiet. Quiet in the courtroom.'

'Black lives matter!' someone hollers.

'Jerome mattered,' shouts Grandma. 'He was a good boy.'

'Order. Order!' yells the judge. Security guards move towards my parents. I collapse on the floor, feeling like I've been shot again. I'm furious.

There's no order. Only swirls of noise, wailing, shouts, and commands. The court artist is sketching furiously. Reporters are pushing, shoving, shouting questions: 'Can there be justice?' 'Officer Moore, are you sorry?' 'Mrs Moore, can you tell us how you feel? Did your husband do right?'

I don't hear any answers. What does it matter if Officer

Moore is sorry? If his wife is sorry? If the whole world is sorry?

I stare at the ceiling. It's painted blue.

'I see you.'

I'm shocked. This white girl is standing, staring right at me.

Mouth shaped like an **O**, she trembles. Her eyes are crystal blue; she's not a ghost; she's Officer Moore's daughter.

What does it mean?

Not cool.

Why can't it be Kim who sees me? Why this stupid girl?

ALIVE

December 8
Gun

Carlos waves the gun wildly, pointing at Eddie, Mike, and Snap. I back away, moving to the left, closer to the hall door. I should've known better. Friends get you in trouble.

'Leave me alone. I mean it.' Carlos scrambles to his feet.

'We were just playing,' says Mike.

'No need to be upset,' adds Snap.

Eddie stares. 'How'd you get a gun in school?'

Carlos doesn't answer.

Though nervous, I shout, 'Leave us alone!' I inch sideways, closer to Carlos, away from the line of fire between the gun and Eddie.

Mike, Eddie, and Snap try not to act scared. Carlos holds the gun firm, with two hands. He looks more frightened than they are.

Eddie grabs Mike's shoulder. 'Come on.' Mike doesn't want to go, but Eddie is the leader. Scornful, Snap says, 'I don't care about some Texas kid.'

'He should go back to Texas.' Mike spits. 'Later.'

Later what? They'll beat us up?

'If you come back, you'll be sorry,' says Carlos.

'Yeah,' I warn. 'Sorry.'

'So now you're tough, Jerome?'

I cringe, and don't answer Eddie. I'm nauseous. Sorry I got into this mess.

Carlos juts the gun towards Eddie.

'See you later, Jerome. Most def.'

'Let's go,' says Eddie, and he, Mike, and Snap saunter out the door.

The lunch bell rings. Back to class. Relieved, I rush forward. Ma and Grandma are going to kill me if they find out I was near a gun.

Carlos grips my arm. 'Jerome! It isn't real. See.'

It isn't real? I stare, whistling. 'Plastic? That's how you got it through security.'

Carlos grins, nodding. Then he laughs, his voice pitching higher and higher. 'A good trick. Right?'

'Trick,' I repeat, doubling over, laughing. We're both sweating, hysterical. I gulp air.

I'm less scared. Still nervous. But less scared. Carlos is smart.

A toy gun.

DEAD

SARAH

Not knowing how, I find the girl's house. It's not a mansion but it's nicer than my family's apartment. There's a front and back yard. A porch. A basement and two floors. Windows everywhere.

A police car is in the driveway.

A curtain flutters. I see the girl. Like magic, I float inside, into the second floor and a pink bedroom.

The girl stumbles, falls against her dresser. She wants to scream, I can tell. But she doesn't.

'I recognised your picture,' she says, breathless, terrified.

'You see me? How come?'

'I don't know.' She's got freckles. A nervous smile. Brave, she stands up straighter.

'It's been lonely. Not talking to anyone. Not being seen.'

'I'm lonely, too,' she says, flushing. 'Sounds dumb. But I am lonely. Ever since my dad shot you. He and my mother fight. They're sad all the time.'

'They should be—'

'Sad? He was scared.'

'I was playing. I was the good guy.'

I *was*, too. Kim and me hardly ever played outside.

'Gangs. Drive-bys,' my parents always say. It was a special afternoon, me, outside, rather than stuck in the dark apartment. I told Grandma I'd made a friend. It was a fine day.

'I'm sorry,' the girl whispers.

Her sorry makes me angry. If she wasn't a girl, I'd think about hitting her.

Dead, I can't hit anyone. And that makes me even angrier. Her bedroom is three times the size of mine. Decorated with a bookshelf, framed pictures, a pink striped comforter, a TV, and a computer. I bet she doesn't even hear gunshots in her neighbourhood.

'My dad was doing his job.'

'He said that?'

She presses her lips tight.

'He shot me.'

'My dad protects and serves. That's what policemen do.'

'He didn't protect me. Everybody in my neighbourhood knows cops do whatever they want.'

'That's not true. He upholds the law.'

I grunt.

Upset, the girl rocks back on her heels.

I don't care. Her bedroom is like cotton candy. Sickly sweet. Ballerinas on the lampshade glow. Two tiny stuffed pigs rest on the pillows. Nothing bad is supposed to happen to whoever sleeps in this room.

'Jerome?'

I don't answer.

'Can I help?'

I almost scream, *Can you make me alive again?* But I don't. This girl is crying. I'm surprised a stranger is crying for me.

'I can't change things. You're all over the news.'

I don't want to be in the news. 'What're they saying?'

'Depends.'

Before I can say, 'On what?' the door opens.

'Sarah, time for bed.'

'Yes, Dad.'

Officer Moore is skinny with big hands and reddened eyes. He hugs his daughter, tight. I think she might break. But Sarah doesn't pull away.

'Want to go skating tomorrow?'

'Sure, Dad.'

He kisses her forehead and I'm jealous. Who'll ever kiss me?

'Dad? Is it true he was twelve?'

Officer Moore holds Sarah at arm's length. 'It's a rough neighbourhood.'

'Same age as me.'

'You don't know him. You didn't see him.'

Sarah looks at me. She *does* see me. We're the same height. Probably in the same grade. Seventh.

'He's—' She points, stops, stutters. 'He was my height.'

Her father blinks, like he doesn't recognise her. Like

he can't believe she's contradicting him.

She plunges on. 'You said he was big. Scary.'

'*I* was there,' he fires back. 'Not you.'

Sarah lowers her eyes, clasps her hands, trembling.

Her father leaves, slamming the door.

He doesn't hear, 'Did you make a mistake?'

'No, he didn't,' I answer.

'It must've been a mistake.'

'He did it on purpose.'

'No, it was a mistake.'

'Later,' I say, disgusted.

'Don't leave.'

'Why should I stay?'

'We could be friends.'

'That's the stupidest thing.' I've never had a friend like Sarah. A white girl. I laugh, it's so stupid. Die, and a white girl can be your friend.

'I'm not trying to be funny. Stay.'

She's pleading. I feel sorry for her. My school doesn't have any Sarahs. Definitely not ones who like pigs and pink. 'Got to go,' I say.

'Where?'

This catches me up short. I don't know. I don't even know how I go, how I move. I just dissolve. Fade away, then appear again. Can I control that?

*   *   *

Beside Sarah, I feel like I'm being watched. Uneasy, I turn, try to lift the window curtain.

Ghost boy is looking up at me. A street light's glow filters through him. He's watching, waiting for something. From me? Sarah?

Next to me, Sarah sniffs, whimpers. 'What does it feel like? Being dead? Aren't you supposed to go somewhere?'

Now I feel like crying. I'm sick. Homesick. But my family, even Kim, can't see me. I hate watching them eat cereal, fake smiling and pretending the day is ordinary. I hate seeing where I used to sit, empty.

Who knew death was so complicated? Who knew THE END wasn't the end?

'I hate school.' Sarah sits on her fluffy bed.

'What? You being bullied?' I understand bullying. Being shoved into lockers. Humiliated.

'Some people are angry at my dad. They shout at me like I'm a bad person. But some people...' She looks down at her hands. 'Some people think my dad's a hero. That he was doing his job. That he's brave and I should be proud of him. That I'm special, lucky to be his daughter. I'm embarrassed.'

I shudder. 'I don't believe it. Your family's got everything. A nice life. People celebrating you. It's not—'

'Fair.'

Twice, she's finished my sentence. 'Later,' I say.

'I don't want to be liked because my dad killed you.'

She looks like her dad. It's hard looking at her. I swallow.

'Sarah. That's your name?'

She nods. 'I love Dad more than anything. But seeing you, I wonder how he could've—'

'Shot me?'

'Yes. Maybe someone might shoot me?'

'Naw, you're a girl. And white.'

'Is that it? Is that true?'

I shrug my shoulders. How many times had I heard: 'Be careful of police'; 'Be careful of white people...' Everybody in the neighbourhood knew it. Pop told me as soon as I could read.

I sit cross-legged on the floor. No bones, no muscles, but I feel tired just the same.

'I'm supposed to see you,' insists Sarah. 'It means something. It must.'

She sits, cross-legged, beside me. Even her nails are pink. 'I think I'm supposed to help you.'

'Help me? How can you help me?'

'I don't know.'

'My grandmother. She tells me it's time to get going. Move on.'

'She can see you?'

'Naw, not like you. She can't hear me either. But she senses I'm around.' I sigh.

Sarah sighs. Two kids. One dead, one alive.

Crazy. I laugh again. Sarah smiles, then laughs with me. She knows I'm not laughing at her. We're both nervous. I think, if we weren't laughing, we'd cry.

Doesn't feel right to be laughing when I'm dead.

I wish I'd never met Sarah.

ALIVE

December 8
School

Carlos sits in the row across from me through every subject. Language arts, history, maths. Sometimes his head drops on to his desk. Like he hasn't had enough sleep. He's skinny. Much skinnier than me. Skinnier than Kim.

I want the bell to ring. I've done too much already. Helped Carlos. Watched Mike, Eddie, and Snap pretend they weren't scared. I'm exhausted. Anxious. Tense.

Today, I wasn't stomped. Wasn't so lonely. I'm confused. Being good gets me in trouble; scaring bullies gets me out. I don't like it. I don't like thinking about how to keep myself safe tomorrow. And the next day.

I don't have a toy gun.

The bell rings. 'Bye,' I say to Carlos. I dash out the room. Lugging my backpack, I rush through the school door, down the steps. On the sidewalk, I wait for Kim. Kids rush by me.

Surprising me, Carlos tugs my coat. 'Hey, let's hang out.'

Cold, shivering, he says, 'I can be late. My mom won't mind.' He's grinning, wide awake.

He lifts the gun partway out of his pocket. 'We could play. Pretend we're taking down zombies.'

'No.' I shake my head, trembling.

'We're friends now, aren't we, Jerome?'

I frown at the shape in his pocket. I remind myself it's a toy. Not a gun.

I shake my head again. 'I have to go home.'

'Then you take it. Give it back tomorrow.'

'Jerome?' I hear.

'My sister.'

Carlos nods. 'Hey.'

Kim smiles sweet like she thinks Carlos is cute.

'I'm Carlos. Jerome is my friend.'

Kim smiles brighter. 'Hey, Carlos.' She's not used to anyone calling me 'friend'.

Carlos grins. 'Chicago's not so bad.' He offers the gun. Kim steps back. I shift my body so people can't see.

'It's okay, Kim,' says Carlos. 'It's just a toy.'

Carlos puts it in my hand. The plastic feels light, clammy.

'Play with it, Jerome.'

'No,' I say, sliding my hand free.

'It'll be fun. You can scare the bad guys. Kim, you won't believe what we did.'

'Don't!' I don't want Kim to know what happened.

'Got it, sorry.' He steps closer, murmuring, 'I'm just trying to say thanks, Jerome. You helped me out a lot. Good friends share. You can bring it back tomorrow.'

Carlos is serious. He looks like a mouse. One of the nicest in a Disney cartoon – all curious, helpful, and worried at the same time.

Kim stares at me. Her eyes are telling me 'no.' *Don't do it.*

The sky is overcast. There isn't any snow, just dirty mounds of ice on the ground. Kids are escaping school, yelling and shouting. Across the street are some dealers. Principal Alton watches them. Nobody is approaching me, Carlos, and Kim.

I study the gun.

The gun's blackness is bold, startling.

I'm always good. (Teasing Kim doesn't count.) I say what Grandma wants to hear. Calm her and Ma. Watch out for Kim. Play *Minecraft* for just an hour. (Okay, sometimes two.) Do my homework. Even act nice when Mr Myers isn't asking me (he's asking the whole class!) to welcome the new kid. Sucker. That's me. Why can't I have some fun? Pretend I'm a rebel in *Rogue One*?

Better yet, scare Eddie if he tries ambushing me on the way home? Or jumping me tomorrow on the way to school? Why am I the only one who's scared all the time?

'It's just a toy,' I whisper to Kim. 'It won't do anything bad.'

The gun rests in Carlos's brown palm.

My head aches; my stomach hurts.

'Grandma and Ma won't like it. Pop will get mad.'

Weird, Kim's words make me want the toy more.

'It's okay,' says Carlos. In the cold, his breath blows smoke. 'It's okay.' Carlos spins, tucks the toy into his pocket.

I clutch his arm. 'I want to play.'

Carlos grins. Slyly, he slides the toy to me. 'Bye!' he says, jogging, then running full out.

I grip the handle. It's firm with ridges. The barrel doesn't spin. But the trigger cocks just as if you were loading or firing a real gun. I look down the rounded muzzle. There aren't any plastic bullets. Or pellets. My hands shake. I look up. Light snow falls. I shiver.

It's just a toy. Why am I scared of a toy?

'I made a friend,' I say to Kim as if that explains everything.

She scowls and starts walking home, her lips taut, thin like Ma's when she's angry.

'Today was a good day,' I say. 'I didn't get hurt. I didn't get beat.

'Today was a good day. I made a friend.'

I keep chattering and though she's my little sister, she's street smart. She knows how lonely my school days are. She knows I'm begging, begging without saying, *Don't tell. Don't tell. Please don't tell Ma. Or Grandma. Especially not Pop.*

She slips her hand in mine; I know I'm safe. We walk home. My left hand feels how warm Kim's glove is. Like Carlos, I don't have any gloves.

My right hand clutches the plastic in my pocket. It burns.

DEAD

Preliminary Hearing
Chicago Courthouse

April 18

'Were you surprised you shot a child?'

'Asked and answered, Your Honor,' says the defending lawyer.

'I'll rephrase. Why were you surprised?' asks the lawyer calmly. 'Can't you tell the difference between a boy and a man?'

'Yes, of course. I mean…it was dark.'

'Daylight.'

The judge's face is like a mask; her hair, silver. She peers at Officer Moore.

Officer Moore swallows. 'Yes, daylight. He was big.'

'More than any other twelve-year-old?'

'Yes. Bigger.'

'Are you prejudiced?'

'No.'

'Liar,' someone shouts.

'Quiet,' the judge warns, tapping her gavel once.

I look across the courtroom at Sarah. Eyes wide, her elbows on her knees, her palms cupped over her head. I'm standing next to her father, studying him.

'Have you heard of racial bias?'

'No.'

'Heard prejudice can affect your thoughts, actions? Whether consciously. Knowing. Or unconsciously?'

'I'm not racist.'

'Possibly you were responding to unconscious stereotypes of black men as large, threatening, dangerous?'

'No. I acted with just cause.'

'How tall is your daughter?'

'Objection,' says the seated lawyer.

'Sustained,' answers the judge.

'I'll ask another way. Would it surprise you if I told you Jerome Rogers, the child you killed, was no taller than five feet, ninety pounds?'

Officer Moore is surprised.

Her palms pressed tight against her ears, Sarah bows her head. She can't see her father squirm. I can.

Then, it's my turn to be surprised. The ghost boy sits beside her. He tries to hold Sarah's hand. She doesn't flinch. Neither hand meets. They can't. He's dead; she's alive.

Sarah sees us both.

Ghost boy extends his hand towards me. Like I'm supposed to hold it? Be grateful?

I flinch. *What am I supposed to do? What does it mean?*

Officer Moore's plump-faced lawyer asks for a lunch break.

The judge agrees. For a few seconds, she closes her eyes. I think it doesn't matter if Sarah can see me and the ghost boy. It only matters that the judge sees Sarah's dad is lying.

People file out of the courtroom. Pop is steadying both Ma and Grandma. Officer Moore guides his wife, hand on her back.

I don't move. Sarah and the ghost boy walk out of the courtroom, turning once to look back at dead me.

LOST

'You saw him today, didn't you?'

Sarah doesn't act surprised. She knows who I'm talking about.

'He say anything?'

She shakes her head, her feet dangling off the bed. 'I think there's a reason I see him, too.'

'I wish you'd hurry up and figure it out.'

'Why do you?'

'What?'

'See him? What if it isn't because you're—'

'Don't say it. Of course it's because I'm dead.' Yet even as I say it, I feel there's another reason, too.

Downstairs, a door slams. Sarah's mom and dad are shouting. Glass breaks.

'Administrative leave,' murmurs Sarah. 'Drives Dad crazy.'

'He's getting paid?'

'Yes.'

I clench my hands. 'Pop wouldn't mind getting paid for not working.'

Sarah's eyes tear up.

'Sorry,' I say, though I'm not. Sarah's not stupid but

even if I was alive, we wouldn't live in the same world. Hers is a fantasy world. Like a TV family in a huge house with plenty of money, food.

Being poor is real. Our church has a food pantry, emergency dollars for winter heating. Last year when Ma's appendix broke, when her sick leave was gone, we got bread, peanut butter, and apple-sauce.

Does Pop know Officer Moore gets paid for not working? For killing me? I want to kick something, scream, break down. But what's the use?

Sarah's dad shooting me is real.

Sarah believes her dad isn't lying.

I run my fingers along book spines. I open some – there's stickers saying

THIS BOOK BELONGS TO
Sarah Moore

Kim would love it here. All her books are from the library. She'd love owning one, love writing her name:

Kim Rogers

Declaring a book is hers.

*   *   *

One of Sarah's books has a boy flying on the cover. There's a silhouette behind him. A shadow-figure with arms outstretched and toes pointed, his body floating on the wind.

Peter Pan.

'This book good?'

'The best.'

I flip to the first page. I read the first line: '*All children, except one, grow up.*'

I frown. 'What happened? Did he die?'

'No.' Sarah's face reddens. 'He doesn't die. He stays a kid. He wants to stay a kid.'

These are the magic words. Ghost boy appears. Just like that. He's *not* here, then here.

Shazam.

God, his eyes are big. Black pools to drown in. He's wearing his black tie and wide-brimmed hat. He's got fat cheeks and dimples.

'You look like a chipmunk,' I say.

Sarah giggles and the boy laughs. A gurgling, deep, rich sound. 'Who wants to stay a kid?' he asks.

Me and Sarah stare at the ghost boy. Funny. Stupid. Funny. Three kids – two dead – talking about *Peter Pan.*

I'm not as lonely. Not as scared, I think. Not as sad as I am with my family.

Maybe being dead isn't real after all? Maybe this is my fantasy? Maybe I'm dreaming? Or stuck in a storybook?

I blurt, 'I always wanted to be grown. Being a kid sucks. Everybody telling you what to do. Trying to be good all the time. Escaping bullies, pushy crews. Cashiers who think you're trying to steal.

'I was going to be' – my lips scrunch – 'a basketball player. Making amazing three-point shots.' (Never mind I'm short.)

'I was going to be a baseball player,' says ghost boy. 'Like Ernie Banks. First African American to play for the Chicago Cubs.'

'Lots more African Americans play for the majors.'

'Not then.'

'When was then?' asks Sarah.

'1955.'

Air sucks out of the room. Sarah's pink walls start to make me feel sick. Even ghost boy's papery-thin clothes and skin glow pinkish, yellow.

'You've been dead...years?'

'Decades.'

I wish I could cry. I wish there wasn't a ghost kid in the room with me. I wouldn't mind staying a kid if I could be alive. I wouldn't care that I couldn't grow up.

I trace Peter's silhouette on the cover. He's really flying.

I thought I could fly from a bullet.

Pityingly, ghost boy watches me.

Sarah's eyes tear up.

'Don't pity me,' I say, sharp, frustrated by Sarah.

'Maybe I can help you? Help you both? Like Wendy helped Peter?'

'Is Peter white? He's white, isn't he?' I ask, insistent, furious.

Sarah looks at me, quizzical.

'What're you going to be, Sarah?' I shout. 'You're the only one who's going to grow up.'

Ghost boy touches my arm and I'm surprised that I feel him. His hand is warm, comforting. It's also taut, controlling me.

'It's not Sarah's fault,' he says. 'Sarah can change. She's changing. I'm here to help you both.'

'You can't help me.' My mother, my father, my sister couldn't help me. 'I want to move on.' *There, I said it.* 'I'm dead. I don't care any more why I died. I just want to go. Get away from my family's pain. From you. And you,' I say to Sarah.

'It matters why my dad shot you.'

'Why? So you can feel better?'

Sarah starts crying and I feel like the bullies I hate. 'I want to move on,' I say, stubborn. 'Why haven't I moved on?' I ask ghost boy. 'Why haven't you? Are you trapped, too?'

'I want to show you something.' Ghost boy spreads his arms and moves towards the window. It feels as if he's guiding me, like a gentle wind. Can Sarah feel it, too?

We three stand at the window, watching night cloaking the world.

'See.'

A shadow. Then, another. And another. Another and another. Hundreds, thousands of ghost boys standing, ever still, looking up, through the window into our souls.

Do I have a soul still?

'I don't understand.'

'These are your...our people.'

Sarah gasps.

I punch the wall. Nothing happens. No cracking or paint peeling.

'Black boys,' Sarah whispers, then clamps her hand over her mouth.

'This is messed up.'

'These are kids killed like Jerome? Killed like you?' asks Sarah.

Ghost boy nods.

I turn from him and Sarah. I look down. Hundreds and hundreds of shadow boys. A heart-wrenching crew. Army strong. No, zombie apocalypse strong. Standing on lawns, in the streets, their faces raised to me.

All children, except one, grow up.

'I'd give anything to grow up.'

Sarah buries her face in a puffy pillow. *Stop crying*, I want to shout. Instead I mutter, 'Your bed is nice. Pretty.'

Being nice is automatic. How stupid to be nice. I always tried. What did it get me?

I'm getting angrier and angrier. I explode. My hand connects. *Peter Pan* flies across the room. The book hits the wall, drops to the floor.

'Sarah, you all right?' A call from downstairs.

'I'm okay, Daddy.'

Sarah's eyes are different now. Frightened again. Nervous.

Ghost boy shakes his head like he's disappointed in me. *Not fair*, I think. I holler: 'Why do I need a white girl looking after me?'

'You're right. But maybe you're supposed to do something for Sarah?'

'Naw, naw. That's sick. Her dad kills me and I'm supposed to help? Who are you anyway?'

'Emmett. Emmett Till.'

I remember Pop shouting, '*Grown men. Armed. Threatened by a boy?*' Grandma screaming, '*Emmett, like Emmett.*'

'You're the Chicago boy? Murdered like me?'

'1955. Down South.'

'Everybody knew the South was dangerous then.'

'Still is,' answers Emmett.

Sarah's chin rests on her chest.

Disgusted, it's my turn to disappear. Emmett was dumber, stupider than me.

I wasn't in the old South. I was in the North. I was playing five blocks from my house.

Why am I dead?

I shouldn't be dead. I shouldn't.

REAL

Real is graduating high school.

Real is maybe going to college.

Real is getting a job. Though I won't be a sanitation worker like my dad. Maybe an electrician? Or a business manager? (Being president is a fantasy. So is being a basketball player.)

Real is making enough money to help my folks pay off their house. Buying Kim lots and lots of books. Not *Peter Pan*.

Real is me having a girlfriend. (Maybe.)

Emmett sits beside me on the church steps. Moths hover, batting their wings at the street lights; the moon is almost full. Fireflies blink.

Sitting together someone might think we're buddies. *If they could see us.*

If they could see us, they might see how I'm slayed, crippled with grief.

They might see Emmett, quiet, head down. He lays his arm over my shoulders to still my trembling. It doesn't help.

Dead is too real.

'For me, baseball was real,' Emmett murmurs. '*Crack* –
I loved the sound of the bat hitting the ball. Loved
running 'round bases and sliding into home.'

Tonight feels different. Emmett has something to say.
I can't help but listen.

Just as I can't help knowing sadness has a smell. It's a
musty closet with rotting food and maggots.

'Real,' Emmett says, 'was going to college. Mother was
at the top of her class. Only the fourth black kid to
graduate her school. She became a teacher. Mother said,
"Do better than me. Be a principal. Lawyer. Doctor."
Crossing my fingers behind my back, I'd promise, "Yes,
Mama."' Emmett chuckles. 'Shortstop, that's all I wanted
to be.'

Mean, I say, 'Basketball. Nobody plays baseball no
more. Black kids play the court. Want to be Jordan. James.
Curry. Lame if you can't dribble and throw.'

Emmett sighs, unwraps his arm. 'I don't know those
names.'

Truth is I'm lousy at basketball. Now I'm getting good
at bullying.

Wish I didn't still have feelings; it sucks feeling sorry for
another ghost.

Emmett murmurs, 'Baseball, basketball. Not much difference, is there? Times change.'

'It's people need to change.'

Nodding, Emmett agrees. 'People change, but not enough at the same time. Or, maybe, people change, then forget they've changed and keep hurting.

'Chicago didn't used to be so dangerous. Still, my mother was strict. "Family and faith", that's what mattered, she said. It helped when I had polio.'

'Polio? What's that?' I'm irritated I don't know.

'Paralysis. Muscles like jelly. I walked with a limp. Stuttered, too.

'I'd whistle. Especially *w* sounds. *W...w...w...what?* Had the hardest time making words come out right.'

'How'd you die?' I look straight at Emmett. Eye to eye. There's a softness to him. Like he's a little old man dressed in a cheap suit. In school today he'd be bullied worse than me.

'Now's not the time. You're not ready.'

'I can't believe this. You know everything about me. But I don't get to know you.'

Emmett hangs his head. The brim of his hat doesn't even cast a shadow on the ground.

'Summer, Mother wanted me to go to Nebraska with her,' he says softly, not raising his head. 'Instead, I went to see my cousins in Mississippi. I should've gone to Nebraska.'

I wait. And wait. Not another word.

'That's it? That's all you're going to say? Unbelievable.'

'Believe this, Jerome. It matters that Sarah can see you.'

'And I'm supposed to help her?'

'Got anything better to do?'

Got me. Absolutely nothing.

ME & SARAH

The preliminary hearing has recess. Funny, like the judge and the lawyers are going to play outside. Dodgeball? Flag football?

It's just a day but the hearing feels like for ever. It's awful being talked about. Ma weeps; Grandma whispers, 'Mercy.' Pop twists his fist in his palm. Lawyers in blue suits fight. Except for a slight narrowing of her eyes, the judge's expression never changes.

Officer Moore's wife is in the courtroom. Kim isn't. I'm glad.

Outside, thousands of protestors stomp, shout in the streets. Some chant: 'No justice, no peace!' They carry signs: Justice for Jerome; black children's lives matter; stay woke; is my son next?

Police have helmets and plastic shields. Several sit on horses. TV stations all have vans with antennas and slick-dressed reporters yakking into microphones.

Ma, Pop, and Grandma are escorted home by Uncle Manny and Reverend Thornton.

Today it's easier being in Sarah's room than anywhere else.

Visiting Sarah cuts through loneliness. Sometimes she speaks to me; sometimes she knows I want to be quiet.

She wants quiet, too. Protestors picket outside her house. Sarah keeps her window closed. Her world is upended. I get that. Sarah's almost as messed up as me.

'How come you, not your dad, sees me?'

Sarah doesn't answer. Her whole body shakes. I'd be freaked, too, if I had doubts about my pop.

'Emmett says I'm supposed to help you,' she says, balling her hands into fists. 'Why I listen to him, I don't know.'

'I think a white man killed him, too.'

'A cop?'

'I don't know.'

Quiet, I squat. Like a flipbook, images race through my mind. Me, playing, turning, falling.

'You said I was in the news. You recognised my picture.'

'That's all. Just the photo. My parents don't want me to read about it. See it.'

'See it?'

Sarah's eyes widen. 'Video.' She inhales, stricken. 'Maybe there's video?'

If there's video, she'd know once and for all her dad lied.

She stands in front of her computer.

'Maybe you shouldn't, Sarah.'

She taps a button; the screen brightens.

'Maybe you should listen to your parents?' I don't know why I'm saying this. Crazy, part of me doesn't want to see Sarah hurt.

'I'd like to see it.' Determined, she sits in the chair, types my name, and pages of articles, links appear.

She clicks.

Seconds. That's all. Two seconds. Me, standing. A police car, moving fast. I turn, fall. The gun skitters. I bleed.

'Dad didn't warn you? He didn't say "Halt, police"?'

We watch the silent screen. Images flicker. Ghostly shadows. We don't move. I don't breathe. Sarah holds her breath. It's like a movie. I'm inside a movie.

Sarah exhales.

'Your dad and his partner just stand there.' Staring down at me. The clock on the computer clicks. One minute. One one thousand. Two one thousand. Another minute. Another, then another.

Seeing myself, I remember lying, feeling my back burn and my cheek, cold. I can't turn my head – it hurts – to see if Carlos's toy is on my right.

I can't lift my head, see sky. But I can hear voices – especially Ma's and Kim's, screaming. I see black boots. See dirt and snow. I wish Grandma was holding me.

Sarah scrolls down. Words roll up the screen.

'The article says paramedics were too late.'

Seeing me dying, my thoughts race. Who recorded the movie? Why didn't they help me? Call the police? Can you call the police on the police?

Staring at the computer, I can tell when I died.

Like rising smoke, my spirit leaves.

Sarah's face is bleak. 'I'm so sorry, Jerome. So, so sorry. If I could, I would hug you. Bring you back to life.' Her body leans forward like she thinks she can touch me. Like she's yearning, needing connection.

Sarah is forever changed. I can see that.

She murmurs, 'He didn't *see* you. My father didn't really *see* you.'

'Does he see you, Sarah? Did he take you skating?' I ask, sarcastic. 'Did he? Or is he selfish? Feeling sorry for himself?' If I were alive, I'd flush red. 'Sorry, I'm being mean.'

'It's okay, Jerome. I understand.' She steps closer. I smell lilacs.

She does understand. I blink. Out of the corner of my eye, I think I see Emmett. A shadowy outline. A breeze flutters the curtain.

I wish I could be hugged. Hug Sarah, too.

Preliminary Hearing
Chicago Courthouse

April 18

'You were the operator that answered the nine-one-one call?'

'Yes. Yes, I did.'

The nine-one-one operator looks like a college student. Red hair, black-rimmed glasses.

Nervous, she twists her hands.

'Did the caller identify themselves?'

'No.'

'What did the caller say?'

'A boy, no, a man was in the park with a gun.'

'The transcript says "toy gun." '

'Yes, toy gun.'

'Did you tell the reporting officers that?'

'No.'

'Why not?'

'Objection,' says the prosecutor.

'Speaks to credibility.'

'Answer the question,' insists the judge.

'I don't know, I don't know. I don't know why I didn't say "toy." ' The girl fidgets.

'Did you know in Cleveland, Tamir Rice also died because officers thought his toy was real?'

'I object.'

'Sustained,' says the judge, pounding her gavel.

'No more questions,' says the lawyer.

'Dismissed,' says the judge to the girl.

I wish she could hear me murmuring 'Sorry.' Her saying 'toy' wouldn't have made any difference.

CIVIL RIGHTS

Sarah's school is much better than mine. I mean, much better than my old school. Her school has trees and a track, basketball gym, and football field. My school has a chain-link fence and concrete where I ran and played basketball. Her school is mainly white. Mine was mainly black and Hispanic. Her school has a library with computers. Mine doesn't even have a librarian.

Being dead, I see places I never saw before. See homes not high-rise projects, schools better than I ever imagined. Who knew there were schools with computer and science labs? Libraries with fluffy pillows and couches?

I wouldn't have minded going to Sarah's school. If I'd gone to Sarah's school, I never would've been late or faked being sick. I don't think any kid at my old school – even the troublemakers – would've minded a sky-blue-painted school with bright lights and clean hallways.

The nice librarian, with glasses dangling from her neck, comes towards us, stops, her face puzzled, then steps around me and squeezes Sarah's shoulders. 'Shouldn't you be in class, Sarah?'

Sarah doesn't answer.

'Are you all right?' The librarian – Ms Penny, her name tag says – encourages Sarah to sit. 'I'll call the principal's office. Let her know you're here.'

'No, wait.'

Ms Penny plops down in the kid-sized chair. She leans forward. 'Do you want a counselor? I can call Mr Stevens.'

'No. I just want to sit.'

Ms Penny leans back. 'Sit as long as you need.'

'How about for ever?'

Ms Penny pats her hand. 'You'd get hungry, I think. Bored.'

Sarah can't help but giggle and I feel light-hearted. I haven't heard laughter in a long time. Sarah stops. 'In class, some kids talk about what a good cop my dad is. He *is* a good cop. But he can't be if he killed a kid, can he?'

Ms Penny doesn't say a word, just hugs her.

'Ask her about Emmett,' I whisper, though Ms Penny can't hear me anyway.

'Ms Penny? Have you heard about Emmett Till?'

'Now, now, that's an upsetting case.' She gazes blankly into space. 'You can research it when you're older,' she says, flat.

'Why not now?'

Yeah, I think, feeling proud of Sarah. *What's wrong with now?*

'You'll learn about Emmett when you learn more about civil rights.'

'When's that?'

'Well,' Ms Penny says, flustered, 'it happens bit by bit. During Black History Month. In history class. Social studies.'

'I'm in seventh grade and I haven't learned about Emmett Till.'

'Maybe you shouldn't know about it. At least for now. It's terrible when grown men kill a child.'

'Like my dad?'

'Oh, Sarah, I didn't mean—'

'But it's true!' I holler in the librarian's ear. 'It's terrible when a man kills a child.'

Sarah looks at me. Then, she looks at the librarian. 'Jerome died in the city. Chicago. The same city where Emmett was born.'

'That's true. But Emmett Till was murdered in Mississippi. Sixty years ago.'

'So, what's the difference?'

'Emmett's death made a difference. His death began the African American Civil Rights Movement.'

'You mean like Martin Luther King Jr.?'

'Yes. But much more. Desegregation of schools – *Brown v. Board of Education*. Desegregation of trains, buses. You've heard of Rosa Parks? The March on Washington? The Voting Rights Act? So, so much more, Sarah.'

'You're saying Jerome's death is less important?'

'No, no, I'm not saying that. I was a young girl just like you when the call for civil rights went out. My family was Jewish. We knew discrimination, too. All types of people fought for change.

'In 1955, Mrs Till was very, very brave. She insisted on an open casket. She wrote, "Let the world see what I have seen." '

'Can I see?'

Ms Penny closes her eyes, shakes herself, then sighs. 'Better to light a candle than curse the darkness.'

'What's that mean?'

'A Chinese proverb. It means I'm going to show you a picture of Emmett Till. I was the same age as you when I saw it.'

Ms Penny types 'casket' and 'Till' in the computer's search bar. *Click.*

I turn away. I don't want to see. Dead is dead. Doesn't matter what dead looks like. I walk out of the library, down the hall, through the front doors.

It's a bright, sunny day.

I hear Sarah sobbing, 'Oh, oh, oh,' over and over and over.

WANDERING

Leaves are budding. I walk and walk and walk. At least, it feels like walking.

I roam, going nowhere.

Why am I still here? Yet not here. I walk among people, invisible, and people still make space for me. Like the weight of my air is tangible. Real.

Dead, I walk, while living people talk, laugh, make plans.

Emmett walks beside me. Just like that. *Bam.* Not here, then here. Next to me. He smiles. I want to hit him.

I don't want to know a sixty-year-old ghost.

I want to go home. But home isn't home any more.

Maybe if I waited, I'd see my family becoming happier without me. I don't want to wait that long.

I don't want to feel myself being missed less and less. *Will it happen?*

I hope not.

I hope so. I don't want Ma, Pop, Grandma, and Kim to be unhappy for ever because of me.

I move faster and faster. I'm like smoke in the wind. If I was alive, I'd be jogging. Running.

Emmett is keeping up. I'm angry and angrier. 'Stop bothering me!' I shout. 'Go away. Leave me alone.'

I stop abruptly. If we were alive, me and Emmett would crash into each other.

'Why were we killed?' I holler.

'Right. Why?'

Another ghost walks ahead. Dipping side to side, swaying. He's graceful. Fly, hip. Wearing a grey hoodie.

'Who's that?' I ask.

'Killed about six years ago. In Florida.'

'Hey, kid,' I yell. 'Hey!'

He keeps walking. Be-bopping ahead of me.

All I can think: Peter Pan *sucks*.

Preliminary Hearing
Chicago Courthouse

April 18

Sarah's father is called back to the stand. He looks sharp in his uniform but he also looks beat-down. Weary. The sides of his mouth droop; his eyes are rimmed red. I almost feel sorry for him.

I stand in the back near the double doors. I want to flee but I can't help myself. I stay.

Emmett's missing.

Sarah sits next to her mom. I stare at the back of her head, at her brown hair, thinking, *Look at me. Look at me.* She doesn't turn.

Ma rests her head on Pop's shoulder. Grandma weeps quietly, huge tears dampening her face.

The prosecutor moves close, face-to-face with Officer Moore. 'Did you announce yourself? "Police"?'

'No.'

'Did you order Jerome Rogers to put down the gun?'

'No.'

'To raise his hands?'

'No.'

'Did you fire from the police cruiser before it had come to a complete stop?'

'I don't know.'

'Yes or no?'

'I guess so.' Officer Moore looks down, like an answer is written on his hands. *Yes. No.*

'Yes,' he says, looking straight at the lawyer. 'He was waving his gun. A police car is a coffin. I had to react.'

'Did you react when Jerome Rogers lay wounded on the ground? Did you render aid?'

'No.'

'CPR?'

'Objection!' shouts the defence lawyer.

'Sustained,' responds the judge.

'Call nine-one-one?' the prosecutor persists.

'Objection.'

'Sustained. Counselor, I'll cite you for contempt.'

'Sorry, Your Honor. Just seeking clarification on the unconscionable lack of aid.'

'Objection,' roars the defence.

Before the judge bangs her gavel, Officer Moore answers hoarsely, 'No. No aid.'

The room erupts. Chaos. Sarah and her mom hold tight to each other. Ma shudders, then collapses into Pop.

Pop tries to hold her upright. I can tell he's trying to be strong. Trying to calm Ma and Grandma. Just like I always tried to do.

Three good things can't be said. Can't fix what's wrong.

'Court's adjourned. Tomorrow. Nine a.m. We begin again tomorrow.'

Angry bursts swirl like a hurricane. Sarah buries her face in her mother's lap.

I can't help Grandma, Ma, or Pop.

I walk out. *Disappear.*

CARLOS

Since January, Grandma walks Kim to school. Carlos meets them on the steps and walks Kim inside. After school, Carlos walks them home. For months, they walk. It's a ritual.

Carlos is a good big brother. He isn't me. But he's better than no one.

Both Grandma and Kim have lost weight. Grandma seems so much older and Kim barely smiles except when Carlos makes jokes. Or gives her pictures. Or gifts like a stick of gum, a purple lollipop. Sometimes Carlos does cartwheels and Kim giggles.

He tells her about San Antonio. 'Always sun. Never snow. The sky is wide open and blue. No skyscrapers. Not like Chicago.' Hands waving, he's skipping backwards, chattering excitedly. He's wearing sneakers.

'The San Antonio River. It flows lazy, through downtown. The River Walk, it's called. Weekends, there's partying. People in small boats, some eating, drinking by the river. All kinds of music. Mariachi, jazz, pop.'

Kim stops, shifts her backpack. Grandma's head tilts, watching her.

'Are you going back?'

Carlos's smile slips. He says solemnly, 'Nope. Couldn't ever. Chicago's home now.'

Kim smiles, then races ahead, happy.

Grandma puts her hand on Carlos's shoulder. 'You're a good boy, Carlos. Think you can walk Kim home by yourself?'

'Walk her to school, too.'

'No, I'm not quite ready.' Grandma rubs her forehead. 'I know it's not good for me to hover close. One step at a time. I'll walk Kim to school. You walk her home.'

'You trust me?'

'I do.'

Carlos bows his head; his toes wriggle inside his sneakers. He's proud.

Grandma pats his shoulder. 'Jerome should've brought you to supper. I didn't know he had a good friend. You like cake?'

Not answering, Carlos calls, 'Kim, wait up.' He runs towards her.

I focus on Carlos catching up to Kim. I like him. I really do.

The two slow, stop, wait for Grandma.

Carlos stands in profile. Sadness cloaks him. It didn't

when we first met. Not like this…not like he's standing on a grave. As Grandma gets closer, he smiles big, bright. Now I know it's false.

If I squint my eyes, I can imagine Carlos is me.

Preliminary Hearing
Chicago Courthouse

April 19

Day two.

'Calling Officer Moore back to the stand,' the prosecutor says.

I look for Sarah. She's not in the room. Maybe her parents have decided the hearing is too much. They're protecting her like my family tried to protect me. I wish I could tell them it isn't working. Sarah already sees me. Better than her dad ever did.

(Strangely, courtroom benches remind me of church pews. Long, hard, polished wood.)

Grandma is having trouble breathing. Whispering, Ma wraps her arm about her. Emmett appears, stands behind Grandma and, amazingly, she lets out a big sigh. Breathes clear, deep. She pats Ma's hand. 'I'm okay.'

Officer Moore slips into the witness chair. He's sworn in for a second time.

'Do you swear to tell the truth?'

'I do,' he answers, eyes front, looking over my family's heads. He sits.

'You thought the victim, a child, was a large man.'

'Objection. Not a question, Your Honor.'

'Sustained.'

'You were in fear for your life.'

'Objection. Not a question. Repeat testimony.'

'Sustained.' The judge leans forward. Even though she's trying to hide it, she's irritated. 'Do you have a question, counselor?'

'Yes, I do, Your Honor.' The prosecutor turns, walks away from the judge and officer. He looks at Pop. Then, turning back to the stand, says loudly, seriously, 'Why was the child shot in the back?'

Uproar. Panic. Stomping. Cameras flashing. 'No photos,' asserts the clerk. Reporters are shouting questions. Community activists are demanding justice. Ma, Pop, and Grandma huddle, cling, and cry.

'Order, order.' The gavel bangs again and again.

Officer Moore's wife shuts her eyes.

Officer Moore looks pained. I see the skull beneath his face.

The video shows me shot in the back. People knew. This is the first time the lawyer has said it, but everyone knew this moment would come. Sarah's parents. The other lawyer. My folks.

'He was running away. Why did you shoot?'

Sound dies. There's tense quiet. Like this second is the most important moment in the world. The answer unlocks the universe.

'I was in fear for my life.' Officer Moore's eyes are bleak.

'You're under oath.'

'I was in fear for my life,' he says, more forcefully.

If I were alive, my whole body would be trembling. Officer Moore speaks (I think) a truth he believes. When truth's a feeling, can it be both? Both true and untrue?

In truth: I feared for my life.

ROAM

The dirt strip in front of our apartment has wild dandelions. No longer weeds, they've grown puffy yellow tops.

I haven't seen Emmett. I'm relieved. I don't want to see him. I don't want to see Sarah either.

I'm not sure how to help her. I'm not even sure I want to.

People tell the dead, 'Rest in peace.' I haven't any. Rest or peace.

I roam, seeing neighbourhoods I've never seen before. Some people live in huge houses. With blooming roses – yellow, red, white – planted in their yards. With cats perched on windowsills. Some houses have painted fences that their dogs rush, tails wagging, barking. (Animals know I'm still here. I wish I'd had one. A big dog like a black Lab or German shepherd.)

Chicago is more beautiful than I ever thought. I didn't know there were parks with swings, slides, running and bicycle tracks. I didn't know there were over a hundred skyscrapers. Or Lincoln Park Zoo, with African penguins striped black and white.

I wish I could tell Carlos that Chicago has a Riverwalk, too. Moms push strollers. Men and women run in black tights. Kite surfers ride the river. Wish I'd tried it. Wish I'd known the world was so much bigger and better than my neighbourhood.

I've stopped shadowing Ma and Pop. It's too painful watching them act like robots.

It's like they got shot, too. They're not happy like before.

Ma and Pop used to laugh, play card games. Fuss over me and Kim.

Inside the house, it's worse. Pop passes my closed bedroom door. He doesn't check on Kim before he goes to work. In the kitchen, Ma, shoulders hunched, barely eats, speaks. No goodbyes between her and Pop. They don't hug or kiss. Just work. Sleep.

Try to forget.

Grandma and Kim don't mind their grief showing. Especially after dinner. They talk about me, cry. Hurting, they seem real. Alive.

I worry Ma and Pop will get used to trying not to feel. So used to it, one day they won't feel anything any more. That'd be worse than me dying.

I wander Green Street, drifting behind Grandma and Kim on their way to school, then shadowing Kim and Carlos coming home. Both ways, I pass Green Acres. I keep my eyes forward, not wanting to see where I was killed.

Preliminary Hearing
Chicago Courthouse

April 19

After lunch, everyone files back into the courtroom. Officer Moore sits next to his lawyer. The prosecutor (I guess he's my lawyer) sits alone. He seems confident, relaxed.

Everyone stands when the judge enters. Her face isn't still. Brows twitch; her lips tighten; she breathes deep.

Something's wrong. She's got tender eyes but as she speaks, her voice is robot calm:

'As a reminder, this hearing is not to determine innocence or guilt,' says the judge, looking everywhere, yet nowhere, 'but rather if there is enough evidence for the State to file criminal charges against Officer Moore.

'The circumstances are beyond a doubt tragic. The court truly regrets the death of Jerome Rogers. But...'

Everyone sucks in air, holds their breath. Stillness, silence. Not even a fly buzzes.

'...justice is tempered by the fact that a police officer's job is incredibly hard and complicated.

'An emergency nine-one-one call, a young man with a realistic-looking gun, a concern for public safety, and an officer's fear for his life are all facts I've considered.

'In the opinion of this court, there is not enough evidence to charge Officer Moore with excessive force, manslaughter, or murder.'

SCHOOL & AFTER

It's May. Dandelions are white now. Puffs of seeds float, reseeding the grass and vacant lots. School will be over in six weeks.

Every morning Carlos meets Kim. He says 'Hola' to Grandma and grips Kim's heavy backpack.

'Thanks,' Kim answers, a little breathless.

I follow behind them. But today I panic. Mike, Eddie, and Snap are at the top of the stairs, standing sentry-like in front of the school doors. Other kids don't ask them to move. They just swarm, flow around them.

I'm scared. Mike, Eddie, and Snap never bullied Kim. But maybe that's changed now.

I howl. No reaction. I can't protect Kim.

Grandma, worried, shouts, 'Kim!' sensing danger.

'It's okay,' Carlos shouts back, and Grandma sways, side to side, her arms crossed over her stomach.

Carlos holds Kim's hand. Rail-thin, he isn't much taller than Kim. He's not a match for one bully let alone three.

Wary, Kim watches Carlos. I do, too, worrying Carlos is going to pull another toy gun.

Even a toy brings cops, endangers Kim. I keep

circling – Kim, Snap, Eddie, Mike, Carlos – wishing I could be visible, alive again. Keep my little sister safe.

Feet planted strong, Carlos says, 'Kim es mi familia.' Fiercely, he repeats, 'Ella es mi familia.'

Eddie steps one step down, face-to-face with Carlos, closer to Carlos and Kim.

I scream. No one hears.

Eddie offers his hand. 'Bueno. Con respeto,' he says loud enough for everyone to hear. Some kids stop, peer; others keep walking, their heads down. 'Con respeto.'

Carlos smiles. Eddie turns to Kim. 'I'm sorry about your brother.'

I worry Kim's going to call him a bully. But she's smart. Eddie can still make life hurt for her and Carlos. She says, simply, 'Thanks.'

Relieved, everyone smiles.

Carlos and Kim wave at Grandma. Eddie, Mike, and Snap walk close behind them. Kids stare.

All four – Carlos, Eddie, Mike, and Snap – walk my sister to class.

Not quite a new alliance. Just a truce.

I sit on the school steps and cry. Not unhappily but happy. How come life seems better now that I'm dead? Not even the bullies are bullies any more.

While I still ache for Ma and Pop, Grandma and Kim are moving on. Carlos helps.

Life *is* better.

When will I get to move on? When will Emmett? The other ghost boys?

I stand, yelling. No one hears, sees me. I yell and yell. *Not fair.*

The school bell rings.

Carlos walks Kim home. He snaps a tree branch, then snaps it again. Drumsticks. He taps, tap-taps buildings, steps, and metal trash cans. Quick, snapping sharp. Both of us like percussion. Maybe we could've saved money to buy drumsticks?

Kim skips, dances. Birds skitter and glide. Even the sun seems to smile. My sister is having fun again. She shouts, 'Faster, faster!' I dance alongside them. They can't see me.

Carlos taps on a trashed television in the street. The plastic cover makes a deep, hollow sound; the glass tube sounds high, sharp. My sister wiggles out of her backpack's straps. She twirls and twirls and an old man sitting on his front stoop claps. Two women, snapping green beans on their porch, grin, shout, 'Dance, girl.' Other kids spin, too. Carlos keeps the rhythm. Enjoying sun, music, being alive, I'm happy for my sister.

Kim stops. Her pigtails are undone; one sock has squished, flopped down to her ankle. She's a mess. A smiling mess. Then her smile disappears.

Carlos stops tapping, making rhythms. Folks lose interest. Two girls go back to playing jacks.

'Okay? You okay?'

Her face is sombre, strained like when we hear shots outside our apartment window. Or when the upstairs neighbours fight.

'You're going to have to tell Grandma.'

Carlos shrinks. He seems even more out of place – again just a Texas kid in Illinois. He hands his tree sticks to a boy with a backwards baseball cap.

'You're going to have to tell her.'

'Yes.'

I feel bad for Carlos.

TELL NO LIES

Sitting on my family's apartment steps, everybody's talking. I never realised folks talked so much. Little kids, old people, the men standing, rapping, gabbing on the corner.

When folks are telling stories, the neighbourhood is warm. It's like it glows, inside out. The streets smell of barbecue and greens. Everybody's got a story:

Did I tell you? Did I tell you about my bad hip? My boss? My b-boy moves? Growing up in Carolina?

Did I tell you...I got an A in maths? About my car getting jacked? Finding a dead baby bird?

Did I tell you why I cried? How I got hurt? How I howled? Found my lost dog? How my daddy got sick? How blue crayons are happy? Orange crayons, sad?

Me, how I died?

Kim's right. Carlos has to tell Grandma his story. She can't tell it. Carlos has to tell how he gave me the toy gun.

Just like Emmett has to tell me his story. But he says I'm not ready to hear it. Is that why I'm here? To get ready?

Ghost boys haunt. One by one they appear. Several boys wearing hoodies, sport T-shirts. Overalls. There's a kid who looks like he's eight. Another kid – Tamir? – with a toy gun.

Ghosts fill the street. Some stand in front, or beside, or behind the living. Two worlds. Grandma is right. *'Dead, living…both worlds are close.' 'Every goodbye ain't gone.'*

Even though life ends, it also doesn't end.

Mr Anders's beagle, Joey, barks. 'Ssssh,' hisses Mr Anders. Joey sniffs.

I think, *Good boy. Good dog.*

It's a half-moon. Emmett appears. All the ghosts watch him.

Was he the first black boy to be killed? Naw. I don't believe that. Slavery was awful. Afterwards, Pop said the KKK began lynching.

Ghost boys nod, step back, high-five. Emmett's the leader. The leader of our crew. An unnatural alliance – young, but dead.

Ghost boys.

I understand now. Everything isn't all about me.

LISTENING

'What happened to you? What went down?'

Me and Emmett are alone. Ghost boys have disappeared, like they know it's time for Emmett's tale.

Neighbours are asleep. The moon shines. Moths flit. It's garbage day tomorrow. Rats dig inside pails, eat through plastic bags. My neighbourhood's poor, segregated. Until I started wandering, I didn't know by how much. Didn't know how much I was living in a danger zone.

But why did cops fear me?

'Are you ready to hear?'

I nod.

Emmett sighs. 'Let's go to my home.'

Two shakes and we're there. A two-story brick house with squat, deep steps and an awning to keep rain off the landing.

'West Woodlawn. My mother and I lived on the top floor.'

His apartment isn't far from where my family lives. Has our neighbourhood always been poor?

Emmett speaks, slowly. 'My great-uncle, Moses Wright, and his wife, Elizabeth, lived in Money, Mississippi. My cousins, Curtis, Wheeler, and I begged to visit them. We wanted to play with Simeon, Robert, and Maurice. Six boys. Almost enough to field a team. Plus, Maurice said he'd take us fishing. Four rivers passed near his home and there were seven deep lakes. Can you imagine? I wanted to see all that water.

'My uncle was a sharecropper. But he lived in the nicest tenant house on Frederick Plantation. It was a run-down shack with a tin roof. But it had two bedrooms in the front and two in the back. Me and my cousins slept in blue metal beds and shared boxes for our clothes. Happy, we didn't mind.

'"Dirt-poor people," Mother used to say. "That's why I left Mississippi. Because I didn't want to be a sharecropper picking cotton."

'"Dirt-poor,"' Emmett repeats. 'A stinky outhouse. An icebox with real ice, not electricity, to cool food. But I loved being with my Mississippi cousins. They roamed. In Chicago, Mother never let me roam.'

Emmett's head falls back. I think he's looking at the sky. But he isn't – his eyes are closed. A shudder shakes him.

He looks at the ground, then back at me. His eyes, widening pools, pull me in like I'm going to drown.

*   *   *

'After an overnight train ride, I arrived in Money, Mississippi, August 21. August 28, I died.'

I'm not on the outside any more. I'm inside. In an old-time black-and-white movie.

Emmett's telling his story by making me feel.

Standing on the roadside, I watch Emmett alive again, living in his old world.

Oak trees arch; cypress leaves hang. Grass is knee-high. Crows soar and screech; woodpeckers peck.

Squirrels scamper. Emmett and his cousins play.

The air is hot, hotter than Chicago's. And though I can't feel it, I can see wet in the air.

Sweat cloaks everybody.

Emmett wears his rimmed hat. He still looks like a chipmunk, but now with skin, plump and fresh.

Emmett's laughing, his shoulders brushing against Maurice's. He likes Maurice best. He's the oldest. The big brother. They wrestle, half-serious.

'Come on,' Simeon shouts. Everybody runs – kicking up dust, stumbling over rocks, running through the forest.

The cousins run to the river. Emmett's hat falls.

I try to shout, 'Emmett. Your hat.'

Wheeler points at Simeon. He's the youngest, littlest. Emmett nods, then him and Wheeler lift Simeon, dumping him in the river. It's so hot, Simeon doesn't mind. Robert and Maurice laugh.

'Let's go to town.' Maurice pivots back towards Emmett. Resting his hands on his shoulders, he says, serious, 'Say "yes, ma'am", "no, sir" to white people. Don't look anybody white in the eyes.'

Emmett throws a stone. It skips across water, sinks. 'You're not my uncle. My mother either.'

'Don't be stupid, Emmett. This is Mississippi.'

'I know it's Mississippi.'

'Sidestep if white people are walking on the same street. Step into the road if you have to. Let whites pass first.'

Emmett wipes sweat from his forehead, muttering, 'Not afraid of white people.'

No one but me hears.

Town isn't much. Dirt roads; wood sidewalks. A few stores with porches. Segregated, black and white men play checkers and drink soda outside. Country men in denim. Women in flowery dresses. Two black girls skip. The day is sunshiny and bright.

The biggest store is Bryant's Grocery and Meat Market.

Maurice says, 'The Bryants sell mostly to blacks. White folks drive to Greenwood. They've got much better stores.'

'Bryants have bubblegum?' asks Emmett.

'Be careful. Don't say nothing,' pipes Simeon, his clothes still wet.

Scornful, Emmett boasts. 'Life's different in Chicago. I talk with white people all the time.'

'No, you don't,' scolds Simeon.

'I do. I'll show you.' He heads towards the store.

'Don't,' says Simeon.

'Think I'm scared?'

Simeon grips Emmett's shoulder. Emmett shrugs him off.

'Don't.' My voice makes no sound. *Stupid, stupid, stupid.* Emmett, don't be stupid.

'Here's different,' says Simeon, fierce, desperate. 'Tell him, Maurice. Folks don't care about black people. Don't like black people.'

'Don't even believe we're people,' says Maurice, sorrowful.

Emmett doesn't listen. He walks into the store.

Not much of a store. Some chips, penny candy. Cold sodas. Bags of flour, sugar, salt.

A woman with long brown hair sits on a stool behind the counter. She's pale, with red lipstick and brown eyes.

Emmett digs out a purple bubblegum from a tub and puts a penny in her hand.

He walks away. Not seeing the woman's outrage.

I see it. Hatred.

At the doorway, he stops, turns, and smiles. 'Goodbye.'

Wordless, I holler, 'Run, Emmett.' Like I tried to run.

Simeon leaps on to the porch. 'You spoke to her?'

'Yeah.' Emmett unwraps his gum. 'Said goodbye like I would in Chicago. Put the penny in her hand.'

'Put the penny in her hand?'

'So?'

Simeon hops, twists, like the ground is on fire. He drags Emmett towards the cousins. He speaks rapidly, squeaking, 'Talked, touched her.' Robert trembles. Wheeler asks, 'What's wrong?' Curtis, like Emmett, is dumbfounded.

'We've got to go,' insists Maurice.

'W…why…wha…what's wrong?' Emmett stutters.

Mrs Bryant bolts out of the store. Her yellow dress flaps.

'She's fetching her pistol,' warns Simeon.

Stunned, Emmett can't move. No one can. They're paralysed.

Mrs Bryant flings open her car door, reaches inside.

'W…w…w…what's wrong?' Anxious, his voice pitches high. 'W…w…what's…w…wrong?'

W sounds whistle.

The white lady glares at Emmett like he's a monster. She thinks he's mocking, whistling at her.

A crowd gathers: white men, women, even some kids. Black people, heads lowered, step, slide away, disappearing. Escaping.

Even dead, I can feel, smell the danger.

'Run!' screams Maurice.

'Run!' echoes Simeon.

Emmett runs. Runs as fast as he can.

He can't run fast enough.

Emmett pauses, closes his eyes, then mutters, 'I begged my cousins not to tell my uncle and aunt. "I don't want to be sent back to Chicago," I said. I was young, embarrassed. I didn't understand the trouble I was in.'

'But you didn't do anything wrong.'

Emmett almost fades, then I see the shape of him, more focused and bold. 'What mattered was what *they* – white people – thought I had done. It gets worse. See.'

I stare into his eyes.

Past midnight, the house is cloaked in darkness. Two white men burst into the shack, guns pulled, flashlights startling, searching

141

faces. Everyone's howling, frightened. Aunt Elizabeth runs towards the back bedroom. They follow her. Emmett's face is caught in the flashlight's glow.

'Get up, get dressed.'

Petrified, Emmett wets himself. He pulls his overalls over his pyjamas.

'He's a child. Not from here,' his uncle pleads, begs. 'He didn't know.' A man with black curls and a short-sleeved white shirt slams him against the wall. 'How old are you?'

'Sixty-four.'

'You make any trouble and you'll never live to be sixty-five.'

Simeon grabs hold of Emmett's leg, trying to keep the men from dragging him away. The second man kicks him. Simeon wails, clutches his stomach. Wheeler holds his brother.

Emmett screams, 'Mama. Mama!'

His uncle and cousins are shouting, begging, pleading on the porch.

Emmett's pushed into a truck's cab. He's caught between two men. One drives; one keeps punching Emmett.

'Teach you. I'm going to teach you.' Bam. *'You talked sass.'* Bam. *'Nobody disrespects my wife.'* Bam, bam.

Emmett's face swells.

I don't want to see this. I pull back. How many times has Emmett shared this tale? Hundreds? Thousands? I inhale, deep.

Staring into his eyes, I am inside again. The film rolls.

The Tallahatchie River glows silver. Lightning bugs blink; fish splash, leaping for moths, flies. Emmett is dragged from the truck.

'Mama.'

'Mother isn't going to help you, boy.'

His fist falls like a hammer. Emmett drops to his knees.

The dark-haired man grabs his legs, pulls. 'You whistled at my wife.' He chokes Emmett. Emmett's squirming, trying to beat the hands away. His feet lift off the ground. 'Who do you think you are?'

Eyes bulge – blood floods his mouth. He's thrown to the ground.

I can't look.

I can't help but look.

A gun.

Emmett isn't moving.

Seeing his body on the ground, I see myself.

The husband fires the gun, sparks fly.

Emmett's spirit rises.

With barbed wire, the men lash Emmett's body to a large

wheel. They drag, shove the wheel into the river. Watch it sink.

Blood stains the riverbank. Emmett's hat rests. Amazingly, it's clean. Off to the side, brim up.

'I'm sorry, Emmett. Really sorry.'

Ghost boys reappear, hovering, studying Emmett's face. And mine.

'For all of us,' says Emmett, waving his hand outwards. 'We're all sorry for each other. Somebody decided they didn't like us... We were a threat, a danger. A menace.'

The ghost boys nod, waiting for something. Waiting on me. I feel it.

The ghost boys are my new family.

Then, I feel an urge. Deep inside me. A recognition.

Injustice. Tragedy.

My mouth opens. A sound I didn't know I could make keens out of me. Terrifying, mournful. Only the dead hear it. My wail rises and falls, rises and falls.

Emmett's spirit blends with mine. Merging, we cry, 'Not fair. I died too young. Too soon.'

Ghost boys scream, holler, echo, 'Not fair. Died too young. Too soon.'

We exhaust ourselves.

*　　*　　*

The real world sleeps. Maybe somewhere, someone sings 'Amazing Grace'.

Is Kim dreaming? Is Grandma muttering in her sleep? What about my parents, all the parents of murdered boys? Do they rest quiet? Did Emmett's mom ever rest? Is she dead now?

One by one, two by two, in small clusters, my ghost crew roams.

Emmett murmurs, 'Bear witness.'

'What's that mean?'

'Everyone needs their story heard. Felt. We honour each other. Connect across time.'

Dumbstruck, I watch Emmett wander, zigzag down the middle of the street.

I wait and wait and wait until the sun rises. Until the neighbourhood stirs.

I feel like I'm a hundred years old. I feel like I've just woken up.

SCHOOL'S OUT

Winter. Spring. Summer.

Every time I see a black kid, I yell, 'Be safe.' They never hear me.

Walking my neighbourhood, I wonder how anyone can laugh, be happy. The streets *are* dangerous. Gangs. Bullies. Drive-bys. Police with guns.

But people need to be happy. Or else 'Be like me,' I shout. Dead. Listless, weighted down with hard stories.

Strange, though, I feel something's in the air. *Like a shift; something I've got to do.*

Lately, I've been lingering on my street. Nights, wild sunflowers in the vacant lot close up, scents of chicken and collards blow through kitchen windows. I wish I could eat. Play. Hug my sister. Pat a dog. Stroke a cat.

Without rest, I wander and watch. See a world that's no longer mine.

* * *

Carlos was trying to make me happy. And I *was* happy for a bit.

If I'd known I was going to die, would I have become his friend?

Truth is – even though it didn't last long, it was nice to have a friend.

CARLOS

Since school ended, since Kim said, 'You have to tell Grandma,' I haven't seen Carlos. I stand on the school steps and think, *Carlos*.

Within seconds, I'm in an apartment bedroom.

Carlos is lying on his bed, his hands covering his eyes. He isn't sleeping. Every now and then his right leg twitches. He sniffs.

Wind billows, flaps the curtains. On Carlos's dresser are candlesticks, a drawing of a toy gun, a sandwich wrapper from the school cafeteria, a drumstick, and another drawing of two bathroom stalls with me and Carlos both inside, slapping, pounding, playing percussion on the plastic partition. There's a silver cross dangling from black rosary beads. And a school photograph – me, from seventh grade, cut from the *Chicago Tribune*.

It's a memory altar. Like Grandma's. Except hers has an upright cross and old black-and-white photographs of her and Grandpa Leni. Grandpa's been dead a long time. Since I was born. But every Sunday, Grandma lights candles and talks to a picture of Grandpa in a sailor's uniform. He looks good in his bright white sailor's cap and bell-bottom pants. Handsome, he's got a wide nose and big smile.

Grandma tells Grandpa about her week. How her feet hurt, how she misses him, how Kim got a 90 per cent in spelling. I'm sure she told him about my dying.

'Folks are going to think you're crazy,' Ma insists. 'Talking to a picture.'

I hope Carlos will talk to me.

I focus. I moved Sarah's book. *How hard would it be to lift and let paper fly?*

Hard.

I was angry when I moved Sarah's book. I'm not angry any more.

Watching Carlos, alone in his room, nothing much in it except the bed, dresser, and altar, I feel sad. I wish he had toys, books. A drum set. Wish I could give him the posters from my room.

Focus, I think. Friends for ever. Always. Amigos.

My newspaper photo flutters. Lifts, then falls. Flutters some more.

Friends for ever. Always.

The paper lifts and flies, soars like a feather, landing softly on Carlos's stomach.

He sits up. Holds the paper. Searches the room. 'Jerome?'

I'm standing right in front of him.

He stretches out his hand. 'You forgive me?'

'Carlos.' The door opens. 'You all right?'

'Yes, Papi.'

The two look alike. Sable eyes. Black hair, black lashes. Neither is tall but I can tell Carlos is going to be strong like his dad.

'Go outside. Play. Otherwise I'll think you want to go back to San Antonio.'

'Here's fine.'

'You still worried about that boy?' He points at my picture.

'No. Not any more,' says Carlos, staring beyond me. 'His name was Jerome. My first Chicago friend.' Then Carlos starts crying. Deep, gulping sobs.

'Carlos, what's wrong?' Sitting on the twin bed, his dad holds him. Carlos tells him the whole story. Frightened of a new school. Bullies. The toy gun.

'Gun?' His dad pulls back angrily, his jaw tightening. He inhales. I think he's going to blast Carlos.

'Papi, I'm sorry. I'm sorry.'

He closes his eyes. 'You shouldn't have to go to school scared.'

'I'm not scared any more, Papi. Really.' Carlos comforts his father. 'Jerome helped. Helps.' He looks at the space where I'm standing.

'You should've told me you were scared.'

'I was ashamed.'

'Never be. You're a good son. Everyone gets scared sometimes. It's how you handle it that matters.' His dad closes his eyes again, like he wants to unsee what he's imagining. 'It could've been you.'

Carlos gasps. He hasn't thought of himself dead. Terror-stricken, he trembles. He clutches his dad's hand. A small hand clasped tightly by a larger hand. I place my hand on top of theirs. Neither feel me.

'I've got to tell Jerome's family. Him dying was my fault.'

'Do you want me to come?'

I know Carlos wants to say, *Yes, come*. Instead, he says, 'I'll do it.'

His dad hugs him. 'A good friend knows you didn't mean for anything bad to happen.'

'Sí. Jerome was a good friend.'

'His family will understand. They'll feel sad, but

they'll understand.'

'Really?'

'*Really*,' I whisper.

'Day of the Dead,' Carlos says. 'I want to honour Jerome.'
Then, Carlos, eyes squinting, looks up. 'Honour you, Jerome.
Always.' *Maybe he does feel me?* He nods.

I nod, though he doesn't see.

'Day of the Dead. Can we do that, Papi?'

'Bring San Antonio to Chicago?'

Carlos nods.

'Sure. We'll honour Jerome for being good to my boy.'
Carlos's father ruffles his hair. 'I know you tried being
good to him.'

'I did.'

You did.

CARLOS & GRANDMA

From the upstairs window, Kim sees Carlos coming. Her bedroom curtains flutter, then the front door opens. She must've run fast as lightning.

'Now?'

'Yes.'

'I'll help.'

'No, it's okay.'

'Jerome would want me to.'

Carlos's eyes widen. 'Thanks, Kim.'

I follow them into the living room. Carlos stops, grins at Grandma's altar. She's placed Carlos's drawing of me next to her and Grandpa's wedding picture. A vase holds a fresh pink carnation. Carlos is pleased; Kim guides him into the kitchen.

Home seems odd, unfamiliar. Like a fading dream, I can't imagine living here. Such a tight, confining space, not expansive like the ghost world.

I've changed. There's no going back. I'm ghost boy now.

*   *   *

'Grandma, look who's here.'

'Carlos.' Grandma stops chopping carrots. She grabs a plate covered in foil. 'Cookie?'

'No. No, thanks.'

'You've got to have one. Sit. Kim, get the milk.'

Sorrowful, Kim looks at Carlos as he uncomfortably sits at the table.

I stand by the sink.

'Jerome used to like chocolate chip,' says Kim. 'But these are oatmeal raisin. You can dip them in milk.'

'Thanks, Kim,' says Carlos, dipping the cookie in the glass she's given him. He bites.

Poor Carlos. His face twists. Just like me and my tuna fish (the last food I ate), his cookie tastes like dirt.

'Jerome should've brought you home. I was afraid he didn't have friends. Jerome was good, but a bit quiet. He kept to himself.' Grandma smiles.

'You were his good friend?' She reaches for Carlos's hand.

'I was his good friend,' says Carlos; he swallows, blurts, 'I gave him the gun.'

Stunned, Grandma freezes.

'I didn't mean any harm. It was just a toy.'

Kim pats Grandma's back.

I'm proud of Carlos. His story, it isn't easy.

'I just wanted Jerome to have some fun. Play. He'd been nice to me and I wanted to be nice back.' Carlos bursts into tears. Kim starts crying.

'I'm sorry, I'm sorry,' murmurs Carlos.

Grandma pulls him and Kim together and she hugs and rocks them. Bawling, the three of them are holding on to each other tight. The kitchen never seemed so small.

I look out the window. I can't see them but I know the ghost boys are down below, roaming, wandering. I turn back to my living family: Grandma, Kim, and Carlos.

Grandma sniffs. 'I'm sorry I let Jerome go play. I should've made him do homework.

'But he looked so happy. Mischievous. I suspected there was something he was hiding.

'Yet I was happy he was being a bit naughty. He was so good all the time. I thought – what could he be up to? Why not let him have—'

'Some fun,' says Kim. 'Jerome never had much fun.'

Wonderingly, Grandma asks, 'You knew? You knew Jerome had a toy gun?'

Kim lowers her head.

'She tried to stop him,' Carlos says hurriedly. 'Tried to stop me. She said you wouldn't like it.'

Grandma caresses Kim's cheek. Her thumb wipes away tears. 'It's okay, Kim. I love you.

'Can't undo wrong. Can only do our best to make things right.'

Grandma goes to the cabinet, grabs a tissue, blows her nose. She gives Kim and Carlos tissues, too.

'Carlos, tell me three good things.'

Kim laughs through tears. 'Three. That's Grandma's magic number.'

Hearing the three talk reminds me of good times. Carlos is in my place. Three is magical. Kim, Carlos, and Grandma.

'Can I have another cookie first?' asks Carlos.

All three sit eating cookies.

I expect Carlos to tell Grandma three good things, but instead he says, 'I'm sorry it took so long for me to tell you about the gun. I felt shame. Kim was patient. She believed in me. She helped me to be brave.'

Blushing, Kim doesn't say anything.

*   *   *

I knew Carlos was a good friend. Kim, a good sister. And Grandma, big-hearted enough to love everybody. The three of them will help Ma and Pop feel better.

I feel better.

One more thing to do before I'm gone.

SILENCE

Sarah isn't speaking to her dad. I don't know why but it bothers me. Bad.

Just as it bothers me her room isn't pink any more. The walls are still pink but the comforter is gone. There's only white sheets. Her pillowcases don't have pink and white frills. Her pink stuffed pigs live in the trash can. Her ballerina lamp is in the closet. She spends hours on her computer.

True, her house is big, cool with air-conditioning. Her neighbourhood streets are well lit. The sidewalks aren't even cracked. Basketball hoops hang over two-car garages. It's beautiful, but too quiet. Everyone here lives inside. Televisions glow.

If my family lived here, they'd be outside every day and night. Ma could have a garden instead of her pitiful plants in pots. Grandma wouldn't have to worry. Kim could read with a porch lamp on and Pop could shoot hoops all night.

'Sarah!'

'What?'

'Do something else.'

'I'm making a website. "End Racism, Injustice." Did you know black people are shot by cops two and a half times more than white people? But they're only about thirteen per cent of the population.

'In 2015, over one thousand unarmed black people were killed. It's awful.'

It is.

I stare at the computer screen. Pictures. Headlines. Articles. Video. Sarah has been working hard.

Does a page really do anything? Make change?

'See, here are links. This one is about Emmett Till. This one links to articles about you. The video—'

'Stop.' I don't want a link to my death.

'I'm helping you.'

I stare. Sarah's paler. Summer is waiting outside. Yet she hardly ever leaves her room. She never plays with friends.

Downstairs, her dad drinks, stares at the TV. Her mom sleeps the days away in bed.

'You can't help me. You can't help the dead.'

Sarah is stricken. 'People should know.'

'So it doesn't happen again?'

'Yes. So it doesn't happen again.' Sarah is fierce in a new way. Now she knows murder happens to kids.

Still it bothers me that her family isn't happy. Just like my family isn't happy. It bothers me that the whole world isn't happy.

'You should talk with your dad.'

'I hate him. Don't you?'

Do I?

Ma, Pop, Grandma taught me it's wrong to hate. 'No, I don't hate your dad. You shouldn't either.'

'He killed you.'

'He made a mistake.'

'He's racist.'

'He made a mistake. A bad one.' *Real bad.*

Just like it was bad for Mike, Eddie, Snap to bully me. Bully Carlos. They just decided to dislike us.

Mournful, I say, 'It's wrong to be bullied for no reason. It's worse when someone has a reason. Like prejudice. How'd your dad get that? Who taught him? You're not prejudiced. He reacted to me without knowing me.'

'He's a bully.'

'It's not that simple,' I say, weary. Mike, Eddie, Snap only had words, fists. Policemen have guns.

Sarah shivers, spins in her chair back towards the computer. 'There are so many stories here. So many names.'

I study the screen. It's ugly – seeing the names, pictures of other black boys makes it hard to forget them. Someone will see my name. Maybe remember me? Remember I had a life before I got famous by being shot.

I step closer. 'Sarah. Talk to your dad. Something inside him isn't right.'

'Yeah. I know. He's scared,' she murmurs.

'Can you help him not to be afraid of black boys?'

Sarah's head bows. She's crying.

'Later,' I say, closing my eyes, disappearing.

I've gotten good at being a ghost. Being here. There.

'Sarah,' I say, reappearing. 'You were right. It matters, you seeing me. Me, seeing you. Sharing my story.'

Sarah looks up at me. Her eyes are real; they have depth; they're ice-blue, sparkling with tears. 'If people know more about other people,' she says, 'maybe they won't be scared?'

'Like you? Like you aren't even scared of ghosts?'

Sarah laughs.

'You're going to tell the world about me?'

'Yes. And about anyone else hurt out of fear.'

'Cops must get scared a lot.'

'But they shouldn't get more scared just because someone's black.' Sarah twists her hands, inhales, exhales. She speaks quickly. 'Some people are glad my dad wasn't charged. Part of me is glad, too. He's my dad. I love him. He made a mistake. But him and his partner made it worse when they didn't try to help you. Patrol cars have med kits.' She stops.

'Why didn't he try and stop your bleeding?' Looking directly at me, she's begging me for an answer.

'I don't know.' Her look reminds me of Kim, how

hopeful she can look when she wants me to help her. But Sarah's got to help herself.

'Tell me three good things about your dad.'

Remembering, she relaxes.

'Dad loves me and Mom so much. He used to carry me on his shoulders. Bouncing me, holding my legs until we reached the pumpkin patch. Or the beach. Disney's Sleeping Beauty Castle. I loved how he carried me. When I was riding high on his shoulders, I saw the world.'

'What else?'

'He takes me ice-skating. Not lately. But he does. Has. He doesn't know I know he hates it.' Sarah dips her head, then raises an eyebrow at me.

'Dad loves being a cop. He wanted to be a cop because his dad was a cop.' Then, her voice breaks. 'He's got awards for bravery. Saving lives.

'How could he mess up?'

'Sarah, talk to your dad.'

'I'm scared.'

'Seems like everybody's scared.' Except dead, I'm not scared any more. Not of bullies. Of cops. Of dying.

I was me. A good kid. Like Emmett, like hundreds of others.

Others, including Sarah's dad and Emmett's killers, lived life wrong.

I barely got to live.

*   *   *

165

Emmett told me that the men who killed him never believed they did wrong. An all-white jury found them innocent.

The judge said there wasn't enough evidence to charge Officer Moore with a crime. But he's not celebrating.

Is that progress?

Sarah knows she has to talk to her dad. She probably won't like what she hears, but she has to hear it.

I see images of Sarah, grown, writing books, protesting for change. Teaching people how to see other people. Teaching her kids (imagine, Sarah, a mom!) to learn, not judge.

'Sarah, make people listen. See, really *see* people. Make sure no other kids die for no reason.'

I want to say more – but I don't. Sarah's going to be fine. She's a white girl but she's not 'white girl'. She's Sarah. Me and all the other boys on her computer screen have names. Jerome Rogers. Tamir Rice. Laquan McDonald. Trayvon Martin. Michael Brown. Jordan Edwards. We're people. Black kids.

Colour shouldn't make anybody scared. Is it because slavery happened? Is that why some whites are afraid of black people? I don't know. *Wake up, people*, I want to tell everyone. *Fear, stereotypes about black boys don't make the world better.*

Quivering slightly, Sarah says, 'Bye, Jerome.'

'Bye, Sarah.' *Who knew I'd make a death-after-life friend?*

'I won't forget you. Won't let anybody else either.'

'You do that, Sarah.'

It's okay that Sarah's still troubled; she should be. It's how Sarah helps herself and the world.

I linger outside the house, feeling restless. It isn't over yet.

'Dad!' Sarah yells, mournful yet demanding.

On the outside, in the yard, I can see Sarah, inside, running down the steps. Cautious, she approaches her dad on the couch. He looks dazed and in pain.

'Dad?'

He spreads his arms wide. Sarah wraps her arms about his neck, burrowing her face against his chest.

Officer Moore kisses the top of her head. Three times.

Sarah pulls back. Arm's length, she stares at her dad.

'Help me with my project?'

Her dad looks like he's been punched in the gut. His face loses colour. 'About the young man I killed?'

'Others, too, who died because of mistakes. Prejudice.'

Her dad clutches her. He can't speak. I can't see Sarah's face but I can see her dad's. His tightening jaw, eyebrows rising and falling. Tears. Mouth puckering. Brow creasing. His face contorting with too many emotions.

Eyes closed, he exhales. Hugs Sarah closer. He kisses her hair.

'Sure,' he whispers, crying. 'Sure.'

'I love you.'

That's what I needed to see. Hear. From both Sarah and her dad.

DAY OF THE DEAD

November 1. All Saints' Day for Grandma; the Day of the Dead for the Rodríquezes.

Both families are having a picnic. Right on my grave.

Ma and Pop look better, less strained. Grandma, Carlos, and Kim are joyful, decorating my tombstone, laying chicken legs and cornbread on my mound. Carlos's parents have brought tamales. I wish I could taste them. His mother wears a ruffled dress and pink flowers in her hair. There's a baby girl in a carriage. A pink headband with a knit flower circles her head.

Carlos's ma is especially kind to Ma. His pa shakes hands with my pop.

Grandma, Carlos, and Kim talk to me like I'm standing right in front of them. *Which I am.* Though they can't really see, know it.

Kim tells me Sarah sent her a book. *Little Women.* 'It's good. I imagine all the sisters are black.'

'Jerome, say hello to Grandpa Leni for me.' Grandma traces my name. Then Grandpa's name. 'I love you both.' She lights candles.

'The Day of the Dead,' says Carlos. 'Your day to play, Jerome. Just one day. But I'll be here next year, too. And the next and the next. I won't ever forget you.'

Grinning, Carlos lays a basketball where he thinks my hand might be inside my casket. 'Play ball with your friends, amigo.'

I just might. A ghost boy tournament.

Grandma squeezes Carlos, unfolds a paper square. 'This means so much to me, Carlos.'

I lean over Grandma's shoulder. It's a picture of me. I can tell by my eyes. My curly hair. But I'm a skeleton face. Big eyes, a shrunken skull, with rainbow designs.

'It's not meant to be frightening like Halloween,' says Carlos. 'Mexicans honour the dead. Skull pictures celebrate our loved ones.'

'I want to draw, too. Can you show me?' asks Kim.

'Sure. It's easy.'

'Take one.' Mrs Rodríquez, Carlos's mom, unwraps plastic from a tray. Little sugar skulls are lined up in rows. 'The Day of the Dead celebrates life.'

It does, too. Sweet candy. Good food. It's comforting seeing my family and Carlos's family together. Pop loves the tamales. Carlos's pa likes Ma's potato salad.

It's good seeing Kim be friends with Carlos, hearing Grandma murmur how she misses me, how she remembers how much I liked video games. 'I'm going to give Jerome's games to Carlos.'

Carlos grins, shouts, 'Yes.'

'Maybe sometimes Jerome can watch you play?'

'I'd like that,' he says. Understanding each other

perfectly, the two clasp hands.

Living, the dead are close.

Kim licks a skull.

'No, don't eat it, Kim. It's for decoration.' Carlos places six sugar skulls on top of my headstone. One tiny skull has my name on it. Grandma lights candles on my and Grandpa Leni's graves.

Emmett appears by my side. 'You're remembered. We all are.'

One by one, the ghost crew appears.

I'm at home with the wisps of boys filling the cemetery.

'Will the murders stop?'

'One day. Got to believe, Jerome. You've got to believe.'

Emmett looks like an old man. Even older since I've known him. His weariness scares me. Though a ghost, will sadness make me older ... and older?

I look around.

I realise ghost boys, thousands of ghost boys, are trying to change the world. That's why we haven't said goodbye. Why we aren't really gone.

'Emmett, each of us has someone who *sees* them, don't

we? Someone to talk to?'

Emmett nods. 'Sometimes more than one. Only the living can make change.'

'Who'd you talk to? Who saw you?'

'Thurgood. Thurgood Marshall. A lawyer at my killers' trial. He won lots of civil rights battles. Became a judge.'

'Sarah's going to do good,' I say, confident. Carlos and Kim, too.

'Time to go.'

'Where?'

'Wandering, 'til next time. Got to help the dead speak.'

'Ghost boys stick together,' I say, firmly.

'At least until there aren't any more murders,' answers Emmett. 'Until skin colour doesn't matter. Only friendship. Kindness. Understanding.'

'Peace.' That's my wish, too.

ALIVE

THAT DAY

Breathing free, cold air in, warm air out. My body dashes forward, back, side to side. I'm running, dodging, fighting bad guys. Don't know who the bad guys are – just bad guys. Not thinking of anybody real – not Mike, Eddie, or Snap. Not even thinking about Carlos.

It's good being outside, playing in the streets. No one's going to touch or bother me.

With a gun, I feel powerful. Like a first-person shooter in a video game. Except I'm *inside* the game. Feeling the rush of air; lungs aching, imagining I'm a good guy. A cop. Better yet, a movie star playing a cop. A future agent slicing with laser beams. Destroying aliens, zombies. I'm brave, bold.

'There. Over there,' I shout. A bad guy. *Pow.*

It's fun. Better than punching, clicking control buttons. It's dangerous, too. Exciting. For once, real-time drug dealers might avoid me. Eddie, Mike, and Snap wouldn't dare to take me down.

Christmas is coming.

Green Acres isn't sad. It's green. An adventure land. I shoot from behind trees. *Pow, pow.* I evade, track bad guys. There's a swamp to avoid. A stream I need to jump across.

Pow. The bad guy is down. I sit, catch my breath. The gun dangles at my side.

My breath slows; energy drains. It's cold but my body feels hot.

I wish I was playing with Carlos. Then, it would be a real game, an imagining. Fun with a friend.

By myself, I'm just faking it. Risking someone might think I'm a thug and want a real shoot-out. And if Eddie were here, despite him being a jerk, I don't think I could bully him. It wouldn't feel right. My family wouldn't like it.

Time to go home.

Movement. Out of the corner of my eye, I see it. A car cruising towards me, at me, like it's going to jump the kerb.

I turn. Try to run away.

Pow. Pow.

Brakes screech.

I fall flat.

Blood flows; Green Acres' dirt darkens. The snow turns red. I can't lift or turn my head.

Shoes...some run, walk towards me. People are gathering. Black boots, two sets, stand near my head.

Sound has been sucked out of the world. I only hear my heart. Hear blood pulsing out of me.

'Toy,' I gurgle, stutter. My right hand opens and closes on air. I don't want to lose Carlos's gun.

Pain slams me. Two fire sticks are inside me. Burning, searing my right shoulder and lower back. What happened? What happened to me?

Call a doctor. Fix me.

It's harder to breathe. Blood fills my lungs, throat. My heart beats...slowing, slower, slow.

I want to see a face. Ma. Have someone hold my hand. Grandma.

I close my eyes. *Feel my spirit rise.*

DEAD

LAST WORDS

Bear witness. My tale is told.
    Wake. Only the living can make the world better.
    Live and make it better. Don't let me
    (Or anyone else)
    Tell this tale again.

Peace out.

    Ghost boy

AFTERWORD

During my lifetime, Emmett Till and countless other teens and young men have died because of conscious or unconscious racism. However, Tamir Rice's death at twelve, like Emmett Till's death at fourteen, unnerved me, because their deaths criminalised black boys as children. It is tragic when adults, who are meant to protect children, instead betray a child's innocence. One death impacts us all.

This book includes the revised history of Emmett Till's interaction with Carolyn Bryant. For over sixty years, there have been claims – oral, written, and some under oath – that Till had physically and verbally assaulted Mrs Bryant. The suggestion was that Till invited his punishment. Timothy B. Tyson's book *The Blood of Emmett Till* corrects this distorted 'historical memory'. Mrs Bryant, who identified Till to his murderers, has now confessed at eighty-two, 'Nothing that boy did could ever justify what happened to him.' Till's death was based upon a lie. Mrs Bryant, his accuser, hasn't been criminally charged.

My hope is that parents and teachers will read *Ghost Boys* with their children and students, and discuss racial prejudices and tensions that still haunt America. Through discussion, awareness, and societal and civic action, I hope our youth will be able to dismantle personal and systemic racism.

My family has always celebrated and honoured the dead. For me, it was important for Jerome and Carlos to have a friendship that extends beyond life. So, too, I wanted to underscore that Grandma's and the Rodríquezes' beliefs were interconnected.

Throughout the world, honouring the dead is a cultural theme. Ancestor worship from various Mesoamerican tribes and cultures (particularly the Aztecs) created the Day of the Dead holiday. More than a million African slaves lived in colonial Mexico and their afterlife may have influenced the Day of the Dead rituals, too.

The Day of the Dead celebration begins at midnight on October 31. Deceased children (angelitos) are allowed twenty-four hours for play with their families. The next day, adult spirits are honoured. Catholicism, widespread in America and Mexico, celebrates November 1 as All Saints' Day (honouring saints) and November 2 as All Souls' Day (honouring one's familial dead). The Day of the Dead celebrations merged with Catholic traditions most likely in the 1500s. The Day of the Dead celebrates life, family connections, and reminds people to enjoy life. Families erect altars to their loved ones, filling them with favourite drinks and foods. Tending grave sites and retelling stories about the dead are important aspects of honouring family memories and traditions.

Believing the dead are still 'present' gave this novel even more urgency for me. I do believe that as a living person, I am obliged to honour and speak for those who can no longer speak for themselves.

'Bearing witness' has long been crucial to African American communities – indeed to all ethnic groups who have suffered oppression. 'Bearing witness' means using your personal and/or cultural story to testify against inequities, injustice, and suffering. To 'bear witness' often includes personal trauma such as Jerome's death and subsequent experiences. Telling his story helps him cope with his pain but provides catharsis (emotional cleansing), which allows him to accept his death and his role as storyteller in the afterlife. 'Bearing witness', Jerome empowers Sarah (and future others) to fight against racial bias and discrimination.

As an artist, I 'bear witness' and hope to empower readers to 'make the world better'.

My hope is that *Ghost Boys* prompts meaningful change for all youth.

FURTHER RESOURCES FOR PARENTS AND EDUCATORS

If you're interested in learning more about the topics brought up in *Ghost Boys*, the following are some online resources.

Rethinking Schools 'Making Black Lives Matter in Our Schools': rethinkingschools.org/articles/making-black-lives-matter-in-our-schools

Mothers for Justice United: mothersforjusticeunited.org

National Police Accountability Project (NPAP): nlg-npap.org

Martin Luther King Jr. 'I Have A Dream' Speech: kinginstitute.stanford.edu/king-papers/documents/i-have-dream-address-delivered-march-washington-jobs-and-freedom

National Geographic 'Day of the Dead': kids.national-geographic.com/explore/celebrations/day-of-the-dead/

University of New Mexico 'Day of the Dead': unm.edu/~htafoya/dayofthedead.html

Author Profile

At the age of eight, Jewell Parker Rhodes realised she had the gift of storytelling, when reading her first book *The Last Scream* to her classmates and witnessing their amazed responses to the plot. Jewell's introduction to the oral story tradition came from sitting on the porch of her apartment in Pittsburgh, where she lived with her beloved grandmother and extended family, listening to her African American stories about family, slavery and growing up in Georgia.

Jewell was an avid reader from a young age, reading stories such as *Little Women*, *Heidi*, *Robinson Crusoe* and the Arthurian Legends. Although the characters were from a different culture, the books showed her environments different from her neighbourhood, and girls who were strong and made a difference in the world. It wasn't until she began university, however, that she saw a novel written by a Black woman. This amazing realisation that Black women could be writers immediately caused her to change her studies and marked the real start of her writing career.

Jewell is passionate about 'bearing witness': using personal or cultural experience to tell the stories of people who are treated unjustly, so their voices can be heard.

All of this is central to Jerome's story in *Ghost Boys*, which is based on tragic, real-life incidents, and fears for Black children, for whom the colour of their skin still defines how they will be treated. Jewell hopes that her books will motivate young people to stand up against injustice, amplify the voices of those who are marginalised, and speak up for those who no longer have a voice of their own. She also hopes to inspire them to share her love of writing by trying it themselves.

Jewell has written many books for both adults and children, winning awards and gaining a place on the *New York Times* bestseller list for both *Ghost Boys* and *Black Brother, Black Brother*. Jewell has made hundreds of visits to schools, universities and conferences to talk about racism and her work, in the belief that the young people in her audience will build a fairer and more loving society.

Dr Jewell Parker Rhodes now lives in Seattle, USA with her husband and pets. She loves spending time with her children and grandchildren.

Recommended reads with similar themes include:

- *Iqbal* by Francesco D'Adamo
- *My Sister Lives on the Mantelpiece* by Annabel Pitcher
- *Noughts and Crosses* by Malorie Blackman
- *The Great Blue Yonder* by Alex Shearer
- *Sawbones* by Catherine Johnson

Novel Insights

Ghost Boys explores several themes including racism, particularly racial bias and systemic racism. Racial bias is when people unconsciously, or sometimes consciously, make judgements about others based on their skin colour or ethnicity. Systemic racism is when racism is ingrained in aspects of society, such as laws and regulations, and results in discrimination. The discrimination manifests itself in many areas of society, including job and education opportunities, police treatment and medical treatment. This often affects young Black people, who people in positions of authority incorrectly assume are more likely to commit crimes. *Ghost Boys* is set in a mainly Black neighbourhood in Chicago in the USA. As well as drug-dealing and gang violence, there are police who threaten many people in the neighbourhood. Life is frightening for many; particularly for children like Jerome, a boy who is constantly aware of his environment and the potential dangers on his way to and from school. For many Black or Hispanic men and boys in the USA, police brutality and systemic racism are a very real part of everyday life.

Racial bias and systemic racism are not unique to the USA. The Metropolitan Police Force in London displayed systemic racism during a poorly run investigation into the murder of a Black teenager, Stephen Lawrence. More discrimination then came to light. Black and other marginalised ethnic groups are more likely to be stopped or arrested by the police. Black people often report that they don't receive fair or equal treatment by the police, nor are they seen as victims. This is a main theme in *Ghost Boys*, where the young victims of police brutality do not receive fair treatment from the judicial system.

A driving force behind the writing of *Ghost Boys* was the real-life killings of Tamir Rice and Emmett Till. Emmett Till was a 14-year-old Black boy accused of whistling at a white woman in 1955. He was tortured and murdered. Emmett's mother insisted that his coffin remain open at the funeral for all to see how brutally her child was murdered. The perpetrators were found not guilty by an all-white jury. Tamir Rice, a 12-year-old boy, was playing with a toy air pistol and was shot dead in Cleveland in 2014 by a white police officer. That officer was never prosecuted for wrongdoing.

In recent years, individuals have recorded incidents of racial bias on their phones, showing the world what is happening to their communities. Many protests by the general public have taken place in support of the oppressed and victims, for example the Black Lives Matter movement, which has spread to many countries all over the world. However, there is still much to be done. Systemic racism is deeply ingrained in society. And while Black children continue to face police brutality, their parents continue to teach them how to behave in the presence of the police to try to keep them safe.

But the novel does have a level of optimism. The reason that Sarah can see Jerome is so that she can bear witness and speak out against racial hatred. Jerome bears witness for Emmett, just as Sarah bears witness for him. Carlos's friendship with Jerome continues after his death; his family joins with Jerome's – two cultures coming together – to celebrate his life.

The theme of life and death is key in the novel. The protagonist is a ghost, telling the stories of other murdered children like Emmett. Remembering the dead and keeping their 'voice' alive is an important part of Latin American culture. Día de los Muertos – the Day of the Dead – is a particular example of this. Dead/Alive is used as a structural device in the novel to separate the story of Jerome's life and the story of his death. The narratives run side by side, reinforcing Grandma's assertion that death is a part of life, and that the living can learn from the dead.

Image from a Black Lives Matter protest

Language and Style

The words an author chooses help to shape the story that we read. This section looks at the language in *Ghost Boys*, the most frequently used words and their significance. The larger a word appears in a word cloud, the more frequently it is found in the novel.

Nouns

This word cloud shows some of the most frequently mentioned nouns in *Ghost Boys*.

'Grandma' appears 106 times; think about why this may be one of the most frequently used nouns. Less than half of the nouns in this word cloud are personal to the main character. Most of the nouns in this word cloud are impersonal and are often the name of a job or role. What might the writer be trying to suggest about family by doing this?

The characters in this novel tend to fall into two groups: those who support Jerome, such as his family and friends (including ghosts) and those who are unkind to him or are more supportive of the police. His family and friends are mentioned roughly three times more often than other characters. What does this emphasis on family and friends suggest about Jerome?

Violence and racism

Racism is a key theme and there are many instances of brutality from the police and other characters. The specific vocabulary choices emphasise these things, helping the reader to begin to understand the scale of the problem and the impact on Jerome, his family and the Black population.

The frequent use of the verbs 'shout', 'die' and 'kill' give a shocking impression of the crimes being recounted. Look at the other violent verbs in the word cloud overleaf. What impact does the use of these words have on the reader?

hurt
die
slam
shout
shoot
shake
kill
hit
kick
bully
hate
fall

Think about how the author demonstrates racism and racial bias in the following quotations:

"Another boy shot just because he's black" (page 22)

"Did you know black people are shot by cops two and a half times more than white people? But they're only about thirteen per cent of the population." (pages 161–162)

'Fear, stereotypes about black boys don't make the world better.' (page 167)

Consider how the sentence structure and tone of each quotation supports the point being made by the character.

First-person narration

Reading the novel through Jerome's eyes has a powerful impact on the reader, immersing them in the thoughts and feelings of the main protagonist. The vocabulary choices encapsulate the fear, anger, loneliness and frustration that he experiences during his life and afterlife.

Think about why the author has used mostly short, simple sentences to convey Jerome's thoughts in the afterlife, and the impact of the few complex sentences in these examples:

> 'I'm stuck. Stuck in time. Stuck being dead.' (page 45)

> "It's been lonely. Not talking to anyone. Not being seen." (page 59)

> 'But seeing Ma crying makes me want to crush, slam something into the ground. *Inside me* hurts; *outside me* feels nothing.' (page 20)

Consider why the writer has used repetition in some of the sentences. How does it show Jerome's fear, anger, loneliness and frustration?

Adjectives

Despite the very negative subject matter, the writer does include positive descriptive language in the book. Why might the author have chosen to use both positive and negative adjectives? Compare the two word clouds below showing positive and negative words. Which have the greater impact on the reader? Do you think all readers will feel the same way? Why/why not?

Positive adjectives

Negative adjectives

Vocabulary List

alliance (noun) a relationship where people work together to gain an advantage

ambush (verb) to make a surprise attack on someone

assailant (noun) a person who physically attacks another

clammy (adjective) damp and sticky

credibility (noun) the quality of being trusted and believed in

debris (noun) scattered pieces of rubbish, or remains

desegregation (noun) the ending of a policy of keeping people of different races separate

dumbfounded (adjective) completely amazed

flail (verb) to wave or swing wildly

gavel (noun) a small hammer used by a judge

Hispanic (adjective) relating to Spanish-speaking countries in Central or South America

humiliate (verb) to cause to feel ashamed

keen (verb) to wail in grief

mourn (verb) to feel or express sadness when someone dies

musty (adjective) smelling stale, mouldy or damp

nauseous (adjective) feeling as though one may vomit

optimism (noun) hopefulness/confidence for the future

picket (verb) to stand outside a key place in order to protest about a person or situation within it

prejudiced (adjective) showing unfair dislike or distrust of someone who is different

preliminary (adjective) done in preparation for something more important

rebel (noun) a person who resists authority

ritual (noun) a series of actions or behaviours carried out on a regular basis

sanitation officer (noun) refuse (waste) collector

saunter (verb) to walk in a slow, relaxed manner

sombre (adjective) deeply serious and sad

stereotype (noun) a widely held, oversimplified idea or image of a particular type of person that is often untrue or unfair

stunned (adjective) shocked by the impact of emotion

superstition (noun) belief in the supernatural

syncopated (adjective) a rhythm made by beats which are strong when they should be weak, or vice versa

tamales (noun) a Mexican dish of meat and corn

taut (adjective) stretched or pulled tight

temper (verb) to act as a counterbalancing force; to make less extreme

transcript (noun) a written version of something originally spoken

truce (noun) an agreement to stop fighting

unconscionable (adjective) not right or reasonable

wispy (adjective) fine, feathery